Trixie Belden #3

The Gatehouse Mystery

by Julie Campbell
illustrated by Mary Stevens
cover illustration by Michael Koelsch

Random House New York

www.randomhouse.com/kids

Library of Congress Cataloging-in-Publication Data
Campbell, Julie, 1908–
[Trixie Belden and the gatehouse mystery]
The gatehouse mystery / by Julie Campbell ; illustrated by Mary Stevens ;
cover illustration by Michael Koelsch.
    p. cm. — (Trixie Belden ; #3)
Originally published: Trixie Belden and the gatehouse mystery. Racine, Wis.:
Whitman Pub. Co., 1951.
SUMMARY: When Trixie Belden and Honey Wheeler find a cut diamond
embedded in the dirt floor of the old abandoned gatehouse, they set out to
find whoever left it there.
ISBN 0-375-82579-7 (trade) — ISBN 0-375-92579-1 (lib. bdg.)
[1. Diamonds—Fiction. 2. Robbers and outlaws—Fiction. 3. Mystery and
detective stories.] I. Stevens, Mary, ill. II. Koelsch, Michael, ill. III. Title.
IV. Series.

PZ7.C1547Gat 2003 [Fic]—dc21 2003002138

Printed in the United States of America 10 9 8 7 6

First Random House Edition
RANDOM HOUSE and colophon are registered trademarks of Random House, Inc.

CONTENTS

Chapter 1
A Discovery

"Oh, Moms," Trixie wailed, twisting one of her short, blond curls around the pencil she had stuck behind her ear. "Do I *have* to write Brian and Mart? They'll be home Saturday morning, and then I can *tell* them everything."

Mrs. Belden looked up from the sweater she was knitting for Bobby, Trixie's younger brother. "That's the point," she said with a smile. "Your older brothers have been at camp all summer, and you've never sent them anything but a few scribbled post cards."

"There just wasn't time," Trixie said, staring down at the sheet of paper on which she had hastily scrawled:

> *Crabapple Farm*
> *Sleepyside-on-Hudson, New York*
> *Tuesday evening, August 22nd*

"There just wasn't time," she repeated. "What with our going off in a trailer to find Jim; and, before that, the fire at the Frayne mansion, and before *that,* meeting Honey Wheeler, and—"

Mr. Belden, who worked in the Sleepyside First

National Bank, had been trying to add a long column of figures. He interrupted Trixie, now, with a little frown. "Stop talking about it, Trixie. Write it. Your brothers will want to know all the news before they get home. Why, they don't even know that Honey's parents bought the big estate up on the west hill last month." He grinned. "You don't have to go into details. Just prepare them for the pleasant surprise of Jim and Honey."

With a stifled moan, Trixie licked the point of her pencil, and began to write.

Dear Junior Counselors:

I hope you saved every cent you earned at camp the way I did working at home this summer, because Dad says I can buy a colt from Mr. Tomlin next spring, and, if you help pay for his feed—the colt's, I mean—I'll let you ride him, sometimes.

I learned to ride this summer, because some rich people from New York bought the Manor House, and they have three horses and a simply darling daughter named Honey, who is my best friend. Dad talked to the principal and it's all set—she'll be in my class at Junior High when school starts next month. Oh, woe! Only two more weeks before the grind begins!

Anyway, Honey and the Wheelers' groom, Regan,

who is super, taught me to ride. Honey was an only child, a poor little rich girl—I really mean it—until we found Jim. He's old Mr. Frayne's grandnephew and inherited half a million dollars from him. I know Moms and Dad wrote you that he died just before the old mansion burned to the ground. Well, Jim ran away, then, because he has a mean old stepfather who wanted to get control of Jim's inheritance. Honey and I went off searching for him last month in the Wheelers' gorgeous trailer with Honey's governess, Miss Trask, who is a perfectly marvelous person, as nice as Regan, in spite of being a governess. And after we found Jim, Mr. and Mrs. Wheeler adopted him, so now Honey has a brother.

He's just about the most wonderful boy in the world—almost a year younger than you, Brian—he had his fifteenth birthday in July—but he'll be in your grade at High, because he did two years in one and won a scholarship to college, too. But he isn't a bookworm at all. He's simply super at all sports and woodcraft. Even Regan says that he handles Jupiter, Mr. Wheeler's enormous black gelding, better than anybody, and Mr. Wheeler is going to buy another horse for himself and give Jupe to Jim. He's already bought him a .30-.30 rifle and a springer spaniel puppy, Patch; so won't you all have fun when you go hunting in the fall? Honey and I are going to make you teach us how to shoot.

Besides Jupe, the Wheelers have a strawberry roan who belongs to Honey, and a darling dapple-gray mare, named Lady, who belongs to Mrs. Wheeler, but she lets me ride Lady a lot. Mrs. Wheeler isn't very strong. She's slim like Honey, with the same huge hazel eyes and honey-colored hair. Mr. Wheeler looks enough like Jim to be his real father. They both have red hair and freckles and are tall and husky. Like Regan, they have quick tempers, but never stay mad long. Regan is only twenty-two and loves horses and hates cars, so Miss Trask does most of the chauffeuring. She is very brisk and sort of runs the whole estate, because, of course, Honey doesn't really need a governess any more than I do. And Mrs. Wheeler can't go out in the hot sun and see to it that the gardener keeps the grounds looking beautiful, or waste her energy planning menus with the cook, and things like that. The Manor House is run like a small hotel, with more help than I think is really necessary, but they all love Miss Trask. She hires them and fires them!

Trixie stopped writing. She could think of a lot more to say, but her cramped fingers wouldn't let her say it. She wanted to tell the boys about the exciting adventures she and Honey had had when they solved the secret of the mansion and the mystery of the red trailer.

"I'll give them the details over the weekend," she decided sleepily as she handed the letter to her mother.

"That's fine, Trixie," Mrs. Belden said. "I'll enclose your letter with mine. Now run along to bed, dear. And peek in on Bobby, will you? Make sure he's on the bed, not under it."

Trixie grinned. Her brother, on hot nights, preferred to sleep on the bare floor. And, ostrichlike, he kept thinking that since he couldn't see anyone when he crawled under the bed, nobody could see him. "I'll haul him out," she told her mother and went upstairs.

The next morning, Trixie did her chores as fast as she could. Her father paid her five dollars a week for helping her mother with the housework and the garden; and, when Mrs. Belden was busy, Trixie had to keep an eye on mischievous Bobby. At this time of the year, Mrs. Belden was very busy canning the fast-ripening tomatoes. It was one of Trixie's chores to gather the ripe ones each morning.

When Trixie brought in the last basketful her mother said, "Thanks, dear. Now run along and have fun with Honey. I'm sorry you'll have to take Bobby with you, but I can't keep an eye on him and the pressure cooker at the same time."

"I don't know which is more dangerous," Trixie said, laughing.

"I'm not going," Bobby announced when she joined him on the terrace. "I'd rather stay home and get wetted under the shower Jim made for me."

"Don't be silly," Trixie said impatiently. "We're going to explore the old cottage down by the road."

"Whoopee!" Bobby yelled, hitching up the strap of his sunsuit. " 'Sploring, hey? What old cottage, Trixie?"

"I don't think you've ever seen it," Trixie said as they climbed the path that led up the hill to the Manor House. "I've only had a glimpse of it myself."

"You haven't got a blimpse," Bobby jeered. "A blimpse is a big, big balloon."

Trixie sighed. Honey appeared, then, at the top of the path that sloped down to wind around the willow-bordered lake. "I thought you'd never come," she cried. "Jim and Daddy went off to look at that chestnut gelding Mr. Tomlin has for sale, and Mother and Miss Trask went to New York to buy me some school clothes. I flatly refused to go with them. They don't need me. They know my size and exactly what I want."

"What do you want?" Trixie teased. "Prissy little blue velvet dresses with lace collars?" When the girls had first met early in the summer, Honey had, to Trixie's disgust, been wearing a dainty frock, but now they dressed alike. Except when it was very hot, they wore boyish sport shirts, patched blue jeans, and scuffed moccasins.

That Wednesday morning it was very warm and muggy, as it often is during the late summer in the Hudson River Valley. The girls were wearing shorts and halters, so that they could take a dip in the lake whenever they wanted to, without bothering to change into bathing suits. After swimming, they dried off in the sun.

Honey was proud of the fact that her blue denim shorts were almost as faded as those Trixie was wearing.

"Velvet and lace," she said with a sniff. "Oh, Trixie, you don't know how wonderful it is not to be thinking about boarding-school uniforms at this time of the year. I still can't believe that I'm going to the Sleepyside Junior-Senior High with you and your brothers!"

"And Jim, too," Trixie said as Patch, the new black and white puppy, came bounding down from the stable to fling himself ecstatically into her arms. "I was afraid that after Jim inherited half a million dollars he might want to go to some swanky prep school. Down, Patch!"

The excited puppy immediately transferred his affections to Bobby, and the two rolled down the grassy slope together. Then Reddy, the Beldens' beautiful, but completely untrained, Irish setter, barked from the woods behind the stable. Patch raced off to join him.

"When Jim starts to train Patch," Trixie said, "we'll have to lock up Reddy. He's so spoiled he doesn't know the meaning of the word point."

"Point," Bobby repeated. "Point to the cottage, Trixie."

Trixie dutifully obeyed. "There it is," she said, "way down by Glen Road where the lawn ends and the woods begin."

The little cottage, which had been the gatehouse of the manor in the days of carriages and sleighs, was so covered with wisteria vines they could hardly see it. But Bobby's sharp blue eyes caught a glimpse of the door, and before Trixie could stop him, he raced down to yank it open.

"Wait, Bobby," she yelled, "don't go in until we—"

But he had already darted over the threshold. And then he screamed. Trixie, her heart in her mouth, dashed across the remaining stretch of lawn. What could have happened? What on earth could have been inside the old abandoned cottage to make Bobby scream?

Then she saw to her relief that he had merely tripped on the rotting door sill and lay sprawling in the semidarkness of the interior.

"Honestly," Trixie moaned to Honey, "if there's anything in the whole of Westchester County to trip over, Bobby trips over it."

Together, they helped the little boy to his feet and carried him out to the bright light. Blood was trickling from his right knee. Trixie was used to Bobby's accidents, but she knew that the sight of blood sometimes made Honey feel faint.

"It's nothing," she said quickly as she tied her clean handkerchief around the cut. "Bobby is always covered with bandages, anyway. He must have fallen on a pebble in the dirt floor."

"I wanna go home," Bobby was wailing.

"Of course you do," Honey cried sympathetically. "But let's ask Regan to look at your knee, first. He knows all about first aid, you know."

"I want Regan," Bobby said promptly through his tears. "I *love* Regan. He'll give me a ride on Lady."

"That's right," Trixie said. "*If* you don't cry when he puts iodine on your cut. Do you want to ride pickaback on my shoulders, or can you walk?"

Bobby tossed his silky curls. "I never yell when people put iodine on me." He started off up the grassy slope toward the stable, first hopping, then limping, and finally, when he caught sight of Regan, he broke into a run.

The tall, broad-shouldered groom scooped the boy into his arms and gently removed Trixie's improvised bandage.

"First aid me, Regan," Bobby ordered. "First aid me. Take me up to your room on top of the g'rage and first aid me."

"That I will," Regan said, grinning. "You didn't cut yourself on a rusty nail, did you?"

"We don't know what he fell on," Trixie replied and turned to Honey. "I guess we'd better go back and look inside the cottage with flashlights to make sure. If it was a rusty nail that cut him, Bobby should have a booster tetanus shot. Puncture wounds, you know."

Honey nodded. "There're a couple of flashlights in the tack room. All right if we borrow them, Regan?"

"Natch," the pleasant-faced groom said as he strode toward the garage with Bobby. "The kid probably cut himself on a harmless pebble, but you girls had better make sure. Meanwhile, I'll wash the knee and paint it with iodine."

Five minutes later the girls stood at the entrance to the old cottage. "He must have fallen right about here," Trixie said, pointing with the beam of her flashlight. "He's got short legs, so when he tripped on the sill—" She stopped. Something glittered in the beam of her torch. "A piece of glass," she said moving cautiously inside.

Honey followed her, and then they saw that the glittering object was imbedded in the dirt floor. Trixie pried it loose with a twig.

"Oh, golly," she gasped. "It looks just like the stone in the ring Jim gave me. You remember, Honey, his great-aunt's solitaire which we found up at the mansion before it burned. Dad put it in our safety deposit box at the bank until I'm older. But this couldn't be a diamond."

She led the way outside and handed the stone to Honey. Honey examined it carefully. The facets glittered brilliantly in the bright sunlight. After a moment, Honey said in an awed tone of voice, "But it *is* a diamond, Trixie! I'm sure! How on earth did it get inside this old, tumbledown cottage?"

Chapter 2
An Eavesdropper

Trixie's round blue eyes popped open with amazement. She stared at the glittering stone in Honey's slim, brown hand.

"A d-diamond," she stuttered. "So that's what Bobby cut his knee on?"

For answer, Honey went back inside the cottage and examined the dirt floor again. "That's right," she finally said. "There's absolutely nothing else in here but dirt, not even cobwebs."

Trixie followed her inside. "That's funny," she said. "There should be cobwebs. It's damp and dark—a spider's heaven. Do you suppose the gardener has been in here recently?"

Honey shook her head. "Old Gallagher never takes an unnecessary step. Besides, he couldn't possibly have dropped this stone. I think it's very valuable. Mother has one in her engagement ring that's not much larger than this and it's worth thousands of dollars."

Trixie gasped. "Are you sure it's a diamond, Honey?"

Honey nodded. "Daddy taught me how to tell the

difference between real gems and imitations." She frowned. "But I can't imagine how it got imbedded in this dirt floor. As far as I know, nobody has been in here since the old days when the driveway used to wind down here from the house. After automobiles were invented, the people we bought the place from put in the new driveway which goes straight up from the road to the garage."

"I know," Trixie said, "and it's a wonderful hill for coasting in the winter. The Manor House, you know," she went on, "was vacant for years before your family bought it. Brian and Mart and I grew up thinking that the grounds belonged to our property. We trespassed like anything, but we never even saw this cottage."

Honey smiled. "You must always think of the house and the grounds as belonging to you as much as they do to Jim and me," she said impulsively. "Mother and Daddy want you all practically to live here."

"We will," Trixie assured her with a grin. "Especially now that I know you grow diamonds in dark places."

Honey giggled and then sobered. "How do you suppose it got in here?"

"Perhaps those people who used to live in your house dropped it ages ago," Trixie said.

"That's not possible," Honey told her. "The stone is

too bright and clean to have been here long."

"Well, then," Trixie cried, letting her imagination run away with her, "some jewel thieves have been using this cottage as their hide-out. They probably buried the loot in the floor; and when they dug it up, they missed the diamond."

"Oh, I doubt that," Honey said.

"Why?" Trixie demanded. "This would be a perfect hide-out for crooks. It can't be seen from your house, and the woods screen it from Glen Road."

"Not exactly," Honey argued. "As soon as you leave the road and go into the woods, you can see it, even though it is almost completely covered with vines. That's how Jim and I happened to find it one day when we were out walking."

"That's how the jewel thieves found it, too," Trixie insisted. She grabbed Honey's arm. "Come on. Let's go back and get some shovels. If we dig, maybe we'll find more diamonds in here."

"All right," Honey said doubtfully. "But it doesn't look as though this floor has been dug up recently. Anyway, before we dig, I think we ought to get some pruning saws and cut away the vines that almost cover the windows."

"That's a good idea," Trixie said, starting off at a

run. "If we let some light into the place, we can both dig instead of one of us digging while the other holds the flashlight."

When they reached the top of the sloping lawn, Honey pointed to the gleaming, midnight-blue sedan that was turning into the driveway. "I guess Jim and Daddy are back from Mr. Tomlin's. You go on and get the stuff from the tool house while I give Daddy the diamond and ask him what he thinks we ought to do with it."

"Oh, no, please," Trixie begged. "Let's not tell anybody about it for a while. Let's try to solve the mystery of how it got in the cottage ourselves. When we cut away some of the vines, we ought to find lots of clues."

"We-ell," Honey said, weakening. "I don't think we ought to run around with anything as valuable as this diamond in our pockets."

"You don't have to keep it in your pocket," Trixie said impatiently. "Go and put it in some safe place in your room and don't tell a soul about it."

"Not even Jim?" Honey asked, surprised.

Trixie shook her head. "You know perfectly well, Honey Wheeler, that Jim'd make us turn it right over to the police. And then the cottage would be positively crawling with detectives who'd find all the clues before we had a chance."

"We-ell," Honey said again. "It *would* be fun to solve the mystery ourselves, the way we found Jim. But it seems sort of dishonest to me not to—"

"Oh, for goodness sake," Trixie cried exasperatedly. "It's not dishonest at all. We're not going to *keep* it."

"But," Honey interrupted, "suppose the same person who dropped it comes back and finds it gone?"

"Serves him right," Trixie said with a sniff. "He was trespassing. Anyway, it wasn't dropped. I had to pry it loose with a twig, remember?" She went on stubbornly, "Suppose we hadn't decided to explore the cottage until next week or next month? Then no one would have known the diamond was there until then. So we're not doing anything wrong if we keep it a few days." She gave Honey a little push. "Go on quickly and hide it. And, for Pete's sake, don't go near Jim with that guilty expression on your face. One look at you now and he'd know for sure that we were keeping something from him."

Honey giggled and darted into the house just as the tall, redheaded boy and his adopted father climbed out of the sedan.

"Hello, Mr. Wheeler," Trixie said. "Hi, Jim." She hurried past them up to the tool house beyond the stable.

Honey joined her there in a few minutes. "Jim," she said breathlessly, "is already suspicious. He thought it was very queer of you to hurry right by him without even finding out whether or not they bought the horse."

"Oh, dear," Trixie moaned, handing Honey the pruning saws. "I forgot about that. Did they buy it?"

Honey shook her head up and down. "Yes. His name is Starlight, and he'll arrive this afternoon."

"How wonderful," Trixie cried, shouldering two shovels. "I can't wait to ride him. That is, of course, if your father will let me."

"Of course, he will," Honey said. "You ride as well as the rest of us now, Trixie. No one would ever know that you'd never been on a horse until this summer." She started for the door of the tool house, then stopped. "They're sitting on the porch, Jim and Daddy. Let's go down to the cottage the long way, through the woods. If we cut across the lawn Jim will want to know why we're taking shovels down there. I told him we were just going to cut away some vines from a window."

"Let's not get Jim any more suspicious than he is," Trixie agreed.

The woods, which bounded both the Wheeler and Belden properties on the north, sloped down to form the western boundary of the big estate. Both properties faced a quiet country road two miles from the village that nestled among the rolling hills on the east bank of the Hudson River. Honey's home was high on a hill over-looking the Beldens' little white farmhouse down in the hollow.

When the girls left the tool house on their way to the woods behind the mansion, they passed the corral where Regan was giving Bobby a riding lesson on gentle Lady.

"Where are those two shovels taking you, Trixie?" Regan asked with a grin.

Trixie ignored the question. "We found out that Bobby cut his knee on a stone, Regan," she said, giving Honey a nudge. "Diamonds *are* stones," she whispered as soon as they were in the woods.

"Crystallized carbon," Honey said with a laugh. "The hardest stones in the world. The only thing that will cut a diamond is another diamond. That's where the expression 'diamond cut diamond' comes from."

"It means the same thing as 'it takes a thief to catch a thief,' doesn't it?" Trixie asked. "And is that why hard-boiled men are called rough diamonds?"

"I guess so," Honey said.

"I'm glad you know so much about precious stones," Trixie said. "If it hadn't been for you, I'd have thought the one we found was glass." As they trudged along the path she said, "I don't really like jewelry. What good is it, anyway? From what I read about rich people, they always seem to keep their jewels in a safety deposit box and wear paste imitations."

"That's true," Honey admitted. "But the person who lost the diamond we found, or had it stolen from him, evidently didn't believe in safety deposit boxes. I can't imagine how it got in the cottage."

"I keep telling you," Trixie said impatiently. "It's part of the loot crooks must have buried in the floor."

"But, Trixie," Honey objected, "you know as well as I do that the floor showed no signs of having been dug up recently. And if crooks left anything as valuable as the diamond in the dirt floor, they would have come back for it long ago."

Trixie said nothing. She knew that Honey was right, but the idea of digging for buried treasure appealed to her imagination so strongly that she refused to admit that her own explanation of how the diamond got into the cottage was silly. After a minute she said, "The reason why the crooks didn't come back for it when they found it wasn't with the rest of the loot is that they got killed off in a gang war or something."

Honey pushed her bangs away from her hot, perspiring forehead. "Going through the woods is much longer than cutting across the lawn, isn't it?"

Trixie chuckled. "Serves you right for having such a big estate. Anyway, it's worth it, because I'm sure we'll find more jewels when we dig."

Honey sighed. "I'll be too tired to dig by the time we get there."

It was so hot and muggy that neither of them spoke again until they emerged from the woods that ended near a thicket not far from the cottage. It was hard work sawing away the coarse vines that crisscrossed the paneless window facing the thicket. In a short while Honey threw down her saw in disgust.

"I can't stand it," she moaned. "I've got two blisters already."

"Me, too," Trixie admitted. "Our left hands are tough from riding, but our right hands are a couple of sissies." She giggled. "We should have kept the diamond and used it for cutting away the vines." She suddenly got the uncanny feeling that someone was watching her and wheeled to peer into the thicket behind her.

"Jim," she said sharply, "did you sneak down from the porch to spy on us?"

"Why, Trixie," Honey cried in amazement. "Are you crazy with the heat? Look, you can see Daddy and Jim as plain as can be from here. They're coming down the front steps."

Trixie laughed with relief. "I don't know exactly why," she told Honey, "but I got the feeling that someone was spying on us. If it weren't for the poison ivy, I'd go into that thicket to make sure."

"Instead," Honey said, smiling, "let's go into the cottage and see how much light filters through. Maybe we've hacked away enough vines."

"Okay," Trixie agreed. Sure enough, they found when they stood at the entrance, that the inside was no longer dark. "You're right," Trixie said, after a quick look around, "this floor hasn't been dug up recently, but it *has* been scuffed."

"Squirrels and chipmunks, maybe?" Honey asked.

"I don't think so," Trixie said, pointing. "That gouge looks as though it was made by a man's heel."

"It certainly does," Honey agreed. "And since the roof leaks, it must have been made quite recently. It rained all Monday night, remember?"

Trixie nodded. "How do you know the roof leaks?"

"Why, Trixie," Honey said. "It must. Look up and see for yourself. The wisteria is growing through it in spots, and the weight of the vine has pulled the rafters away from the ridgepole. You can see the sunlight shining through the cracks."

"So you can," Trixie said thoughtfully. "The floor

must have been pretty wet after Monday night's rain. So the heelmark, if that's what it is, was made after that."

"Uh-huh," Honey said thoughtfully. "And whoever dropped the diamond must have dropped it yesterday or last night when the floor was still muddy. We wouldn't have seen it if the floor hadn't dried out since the rain. That's why he *didn't* see it when he left." She shivered. "I wish we hadn't found it, Trixie. He'll be back, don't worry."

"Did you hide it in a good safe place?" Trixie asked.

Honey nodded. "In my jewel box on my dressing table. It's got a little secret compartment in the bottom. Nobody knows about it but me. I found it accidentally. The box is an antique; it belonged to my great-great-grandmother." She frowned unhappily. "I hate having something that doesn't belong to me, Trixie. Let's put the diamond back into that little hole where we found it. Then, when whoever lost it comes back, he'll find it and go away from here."

Trixie stared at her. "Now, *you're* crazy with the heat, Honey Wheeler. That would be aiding and abetting a criminal."

"How do you know a criminal dropped it?" Honey demanded defensively.

"Because," Trixie told her, "honest people don't

sneak into abandoned cottages. Honest people don't trespass."

Honey giggled. "You admitted yourself, Trixie, that you and your brothers wandered all over our place before we bought it."

Trixie blushed. "That's different. I'll admit that a kid might have come in here out of curiosity, but kids don't go exploring with big diamonds in their pockets." She added thoughtfully, "I think I know what happened. Fruit pickers are traveling north all along the river now, getting jobs helping farmers harvest their tomatoes. One of them may have spent last night here."

Honey sniffed. "A fruit picker carrying a big diamond in the pocket of his overalls?"

Trixie's cheeks flamed under her tan. "What I meant was that the fruit tramp might have stolen the diamond from the last farmer he worked for. He might have been harvesting peaches in Georgia and hitchhiked his way up here, planning to pawn the diamond in a town so far away that nobody would suspect him of theft."

"Why, Trixie," Honey cried admiringly. "How smart you are! That makes a lot of sense. People who own big commercial orchards are rich enough to have diamonds. And think how easy it would have been for the tramp to take the pit out of the peach and slip the diamond inside. What a perfect hiding place!" She stopped suddenly and put her finger to her lips.

Both girls stood motionless as statues, and then Trixie heard it. A twig snapped in the thicket outside the open window. From the woods on the hill behind the Manor House came the sound of barking dogs. Reddy and Patch were on the trail of something—or someone.

Trixie tiptoed to the window, listening. Leaves rustled; there was the soft whisper of crisscrossing branches being stealthily parted. Then, as the dogs' excited barking told her that they were racing down toward the cottage, she heard the sound of hurrying feet on the pine needle carpet of the woods.

"Just as I thought," Trixie said to Honey. "Someone was in the thicket all the time, listening to every word we said, until the dogs frightened him away." She grabbed Honey's arm. "Come on. Let's try to find out who it was!"

Chapter 3
A Warning

Honey hung back, her huge hazel eyes wide with fright. "Oh, no, Trixie," she begged. "If it's the tramp who stole the diamond, he might be dangerous. Let the dogs find him."

"They won't," Trixie cried impatiently. "Jim just whistled to them, and they've gone off toward the house." She let go of Honey's slim arm and raced out of the cottage and into the woods. After stumbling a few steps, she realized how hopeless it would be to try to find the eavesdropper, so she came back to where Honey was standing on the door sill of the cottage.

"You dashed right through the poison ivy," Honey said, shaking her head. "You'd better hurry up to the house and take a hot shower and lather yourself with laundry soap."

"I guess I'd better," Trixie admitted ruefully, staring at her bare arms and legs. "But I sure would like to know who was spying on us."

As they climbed the front steps to the wide veranda that encircled the ground floor of the Manor House, Jim called to them from the garage. "What cooks, girls?"

"Poison ivy," Trixie said. "I forgot to be careful, as usual, so now I've got to scrub."

"Will you ever learn?" he demanded, grinning.

"Something wrong with the sedan?" Honey asked him. "We saw you poking under the hood."

Jim nodded. "A knock in the motor. It would take a better trouble-shooter than I am to find out what causes it. I was just going to get Regan."

He walked on toward the corral, and the girls hurried up to Honey's suite. While Trixie showered, Honey perched on the window sill and said, "Regan is no more of a detective when it comes to the mystery of what makes a motor tick than Jim is. Miss Trask can put her finger on the trouble, but she can't always fix it."

"She's very handy with a bobby pin and a spark plug," Trixie said from behind the shower curtain. "But she doesn't know the difference between a snaffle bit and a curb."

"I know," Honey said. "It's funny how people who love horses seem to hate motors, and vice versa." She went into her bedroom and came back with a clean pair of shorts and a matching halter. "You mustn't put on those contaminated clothes you were wearing when you dashed into the woods. I gave them to Celia and told her to get the laundress to wash them."

"I'm a nuisance," Trixie said as she dressed. "Where are my moccasins?"

"Here comes Celia with them now," Honey said. "I asked her to clean them with kerosene, just to be on the safe side."

"Oh, thanks, Celia," Trixie said to the dainty blond maid. "Sorry I caused you so much extra trouble."

"No trouble at all, Trixie," Celia said. "The only trouble with this place is that we have all the help we need except a chauffeur. Miss Trask is always driving somebody someplace just when we need her downstairs."

"What's happening downstairs, Celia?" Honey asked. "The cook quit again?"

"No, Winnie simply wants to go home," Celia said. "She's only supposed to work from nine to twelve, you know, and the noon whistle will blow at any minute. The station wagon and the sedan won't run, and Madam and Miss Trask have the Ford." She sighed. "I'm glad I live in. Winnie's husband comes home for lunch and she's having a fit."

The noon whistle blew then, and Honey said, "I'll call up and order a taxi for Winnie, Celia."

Celia shrugged. "Taxis, taxis, taxis. We spend

enough money on them to pay the salary of a good chauffeur—not to mention the garage bills. Not that it's any of my business," she added, flushing.

Honey called for a cab to be sent out from Sleepyside right away. As she hung up the phone, she said, "You're right, Celia. We do need a chauffeur, especially now that Regan will have another horse to take care of. I'll talk to Miss Trask and Daddy about it." She smiled at the pretty maid. "Maybe you know somebody in the village who would like the job."

"I don't at the moment," Celia told her. "But I'll ask around this afternoon. It's my day off—after I serve lunch, you know." She hurried away.

"Stay for lunch, Trixie," Honey begged. "Bobby can stay, too; then your mother can just keep right on canning tomatoes without interruption."

"I'll call up and ask her," Trixie said, reaching for the phone. "She should love the idea of having the kitchen to herself all day."

Mrs. Belden did approve. "Watch Bobby's table manners," she warned Trixie. "Don't let him eat with his fingers."

"I'll try," Trixie said and added to Honey, "I'd better go get Bobby from Regan now. He's had him in his hair long enough."

"Oh, Regan doesn't mind," Honey assured her as they left the house. "He loves kids. And, look, Jim's got Bobby in his hair now."

Trixie laughed. Bobby was riding on Jim's broad shoulders, his plump hands clutched in Jim's crisp red hair. Jim galloped over to the lawn and gently tumbled Bobby over his head. The little boy rolled down the slope, shrieking with laughter.

Jim joined the girls on the veranda. "Don't go near the garage," he said. "Regan is telling the sedan's fan belt what he thinks of it. My, what a temper that red-headed man has!"

Honey chuckled. "All the men on this place have red hair and tempers and know nothing about automobiles and all about horses and dogs. Where's Daddy?"

"He's upstairs in Regan's room over the garage telephoning for help." He grinned. "This is the third time this week that we've had to send to town for a mechanic. And each time the trouble has always been some simple thing anyone but Dad, me, or Regan could fix."

"Never mind," Trixie said soothingly. "When you go to High, they'll give you driving lessons and teach you the mystery of what makes a car run. Brian learned so much last year that he'll be able to get a license when he's sixteen in October."

"He's lucky," Jim said. "They didn't give driving lessons at the school I went to upstate." He sat between them on the glider. "Tell us about your brothers, Trixie. Honey and I can't wait to meet them."

"Well," Trixie began, "Mart is supposed to look so much like me that everyone thinks we're twins, except that he's a couple of inches taller. And actually, we are twins for the whole month of May."

"What do you mean?" Honey asked.

Trixie laughed. "I'll be fourteen next May first, and Mart won't be fifteen until June first. We're exactly eleven months apart. He and I and Bobby are blond like Mother, but Brian is dark like Dad. He has thick, wavy hair and black, black eyes, and he's going to be a doctor, so he studies hard and is interested in anything that has to do with medicine."

"Gee, that's swell," Jim said enthusiastically. "Maybe, when I have my camp for boys, Brian will be the resident doctor."

"Oh, wouldn't that be wonderful!" Honey cried excitedly. "And isn't it marvelous that your dream of an outdoor school for orphan boys is going to come true, Jim? Why, you have enough money to start right now!"

He chuckled. "Enough money, but not enough education. I won't be ready to teach until about the same time Brian is ready to practice medicine. I want to get a Ph.D. first." He turned to Trixie. "What's Mart's ambition, or like you, hasn't he got any?"

"I have so got an ambition," Trixie told him, with a toss of her head. "It's all settled. Honey and I are going to be private detectives, aren't we, Honey?"

Jim hooted with laughter. "And call your agency Moll Dicks, Incorporated, I suppose. I can just see your business cards," he went on gaily. " 'When the FBI gives up, we take over,' printed in red."

Honey and Trixie couldn't help laughing, too. When they subsided, Trixie said, "You've got to admit that we were pretty smart about finding you, Jim Frayne."

"That you were," he admitted. "Are you two really serious about being detectives?"

"We're working on a ca—" Honey began, and Trixie promptly was overcome by a fit of coughing. Just then Celia appeared to announce lunch.

"Saved by a dinner bell," Trixie told Honey as they groomed their horses after their evening ride. "Do you realize that you almost told Jim we were working on a case?"

"I know," Honey admitted shamefacedly. "But I do wish you'd let me tell him about that diamond."

36

Trixie led Lady into her stall and slipped off the halter. "Don't mention a word of it to Jim," she said. "We'll solve the mystery ourselves, and then he won't dare make fun of our ambition. Moll Dicks, Incorporated," she sniffed. "Honestly, Jim is a worse tease than Mart."

"But he's so smart," Honey protested, giving Strawberry a good-night pat on the nose.

"That's right," Trixie agreed. "But girls can be just as smart as boys, and there's no reason why women detectives shouldn't be even better than men. It's a known fact that women notice little things more than men do."

"That's true," Honey admitted. "I'll bet Jim couldn't tell you what Mother was wearing at dinner."

"What was she wearing?" Trixie asked. "Let's see how good you are."

"A long white linen gown with a bolero jacket and a wide green sash which matched her slippers and the ribbon in her hair," Honey said. "She wore tiny coral cameo earrings and a ring from the same set."

"Here comes Jim, now," Trixie whispered. "Let's see how good *he* is." When Jim came into the tack room, she said, "We're playing a game, genius. Can you tell us what Mrs. Wheeler was wearing this evening before she and Mr. Wheeler left for the party?"

Jim frowned. "She was wearing a dress," he began.

Trixie hooted. "*That* even I knew although I wasn't here at the time. What else? What color? What jewelry?"

Jim pretended to be very busy inspecting the throat latch of a bridle hanging on the wall. "A pale blue dress," he said after a while. "A short blue dress with white shoes and no jewelry."

The girls hugged each other ecstatically, almost hysterical with laughter. "Great," Trixie chortled. "Wonderful, my dear Sherlock. You'll never get a driver's license. You can't see and you're color blind."

"That's right," Honey added with a giggle. "Don't ever call us Moll Dicks again."

"Phooey to you two," Jim said cheerfully. "I'll give you a real test. There's a strange car parked by the garage, and the driver is standing beside it, talking to Regan. Go out and take a good look at the car and the driver and then come back and tell me what you saw. I'll time you," he said, pushing his cuff away from his wrist watch. "One minute!"

The girls hurried to the stable door and stood there staring as hard as they could. Although it was almost nine, with daylight saving time in effect, it was still light enough to see everything very distinctly.

"Time!" Jim yelled, and they came back to the tack room. "Sleuth Belden first," he said, pointing to Trixie.

"The car," Trixie said, "is an old Buick."

"I think it's a Packard," Honey interrupted.

Jim snorted. "It's a Chrysler. Color, model, and year, please."

"It's about ten years old," Trixie said. "A black, four-door sedan."

Honey gasped. "Why, Trixie! It's a dark-blue coupe."

"You're both half-right," Jim said with a superior smile. "Describe the driver."

"That's easy," Trixie said. "He's tall and skinny and pale. Sort of weasel-ish."

Honey stared at her. "I didn't get that impression at all. He's tall, yes, but slender and very blond. Not pale and skinny. I thought he was very nice-looking."

"That's good," Jim said, "because I think he's going to be our new chauffeur."

"My goodness," Honey said smiling. "Celia is certainly a fast worker. I told her to ask around the village this afternoon and try to find someone who'd like the job. Do you think Regan will hire him, Jim?"

"Regan," Jim said, grinning, "loves him. Adores

him. The mechanics Dad telephoned to come out and fix the sedan didn't show up, and Regan was still fussing with the motor when the blond guy appeared on the scene. He fixed it in a matter of minutes. It positively purrs now. It and Regan are both purring."

"Then it's as good as settled," Honey said. "Thank goodness. Maybe, now that he won't have to go near the garage except to climb the stairs to his room on top, Regan won't make us groom the horses and clean the tack every single time. It gets tiresome."

"Lazy," Jim teased. "And don't count your chickens before they're hatched. Even in the mood he's in now, Regan was cautious enough to tell the guy he'd have to bring letters of recommendation tomorrow before Dad would hire him."

Honey giggled. "I know why Regan said that. He wants to get the man back, so he can give the Ford a going-over. He probably would have made him do it right now if Mother and Daddy hadn't driven off in it. There's something about the clutch that seems to baffle everyone."

"You rich people are so helpless," Trixie said with a laugh. "We have an ancient Ford roadster and a station wagon. They don't even baffle Moms. She's like Miss Trask—very handy with a bobby pin."

Jim set his jaw stubbornly. "I'm going to learn all about cars this fall even if I have to give up riding to do it." He strode off.

Honey sighed. "It really makes Jim mad when you call us rich people, Trixie. You shouldn't do it. He wasn't rich until this summer."

Trixie bit her lip. "I was only kidding. Neither of you acts like snobbish rich boys and girls I've known. I think Jim got mad because he thought I was insulting him when I said Moms was good with cars, implying that he isn't."

Honey replaced the top on a can of saddle soap. "I don't think he was really mad," she said. "But he does hate the idea of being helpless about anything. He's always been so independent and knows how to take care of himself anywhere, except when it comes to cars."

"I'm sorry," Trixie said. "If only I could learn to think before I blurt out cute remarks which aren't cute to anyone but me."

"Never mind," Honey said consolingly. "Our new chauffeur will teach Jim everything in no time. Jim's so smart he'll learn very quickly. Why, just think, he'll be barely sixteen when he goes to college next fall."

"I know," Trixie said. "He must have skipped a grade somewhere along the line besides doing two years of High in one. Brian skipped the third grade; that's why he'll graduate next June, too."

Honey smiled. "You and I'll be old ladies of eighteen when we get out of High."

"I may be older than that," Trixie said mournfully. "I may never even get out of Junior High if the math is anything like Mart said it was last year. Dad had to help him with his homework a lot. And you should have heard Mart moan and groan. Dad would only explain the theory; he wouldn't help him get the right answers."

"I'm counting on Miss Trask," Honey said as they walked out of the stable, arm in arm. "Thank goodness she was a math instructor before she came to us."

"We've just got to be good in math if we're going to be detectives," Trixie said. "Brian says FBI men are all lawyers or certified public accountants. If we're going to compete with CPA's, we've got to be super mathematicians."

"We're not starting out in a very super way," Honey said, pointing toward the garage. "Look at our new chauffeur's car. It's neither black nor dark-blue. It's a very dirty green. I'll bet Jim could have rattled off the license number after one quick look."

"Your new chauffeur," Trixie said thoughtfully,

"certainly knows how to drive. Look at the way he's backing and turning without even getting near the hollyhocks. Regan generally bruises a few when he does it."

They watched the car disappear down the driveway; then Regan called to them. "How do you like that?" he asked when they joined him. "A wizard under the hood and an expert behind the wheel. Do you think your dad will hire him, Honey? I could use a guy like that around here."

"I'm sure he will," Honey said. "We were all talking about it at dinner this evening—how much we needed a chauffeur so you could spend all your time with the horses, Regan."

"We need a new gardener, too," Regan said, narrowing his eyes. "Gallagher quit. Said somebody made off with his pruning saws and shovels."

"Oh, heavens," Honey moaned. "We forgot and left them down at the cottage."

"What cottage?" Regan demanded suspiciously.

"It used to be the gatehouse," Honey explained, "when the old driveway circled down to Glen Road. Trixie and I were exploring it this morning."

"What next?" he asked wearily. "Exploring with pruning saws and shovels?"

"We had to let in some light," Trixie hastily explained. "So we cut away the vines from one window."

"Nothing surprises me any more," Regan said with a slow grin. "And I suppose the shovels were used to dig up buried treasure?"

"That's right," Trixie said quickly, grinning back at him. "We'd better go and get the tools right now, Honey."

"We certainly had," Honey agreed. "We're going to get an awful scolding from Miss Trask if Gallagher really quit. He was the only gardener she could find who had a car of his own, so he could drive himself back and forth." She smiled sweetly at Regan. "Now that we're going to have a chauffeur, I suppose that's not important any more. He'll have plenty of time to drive the help back and forth."

Regan guffawed. "He won't have time for much else. What with a cook, a laundress, and three maids. The cook and Celia sleep in, but they've got to be toted in and out on their days off. And it seems to me that no sooner do the others arrive than it's time to take 'em back."

"I know," Honey cried sympathetically. "It's been awfully hard for you and Miss Trask, Regan, with all the other things you have to do. But everything will be fine now that we're going to have a chauffeur."

They said good night and hurried away toward the cottage. "I'm glad we're poor," Trixie said. "The servant problem would drive me mad. Miss Trask is going to be cross as anything if Gallagher quit, and I'm going to get the dickens for coming home after nine. All because of servants."

"You don't have to help me bring the stuff back to the tool house," Honey cried. "I can manage."

Trixie shook her head. "It's beginning to grow dark, and I don't think you should go down there by yourself."

Honey stopped short in amazement. "Why on earth not? Since when did you get so cautious, Trixie?"

"I don't want to scare you, Honey," Trixie said thoughtfully. "But someone heard us talking this morning. Whoever was eavesdropping in the thicket knows that you have a valuable diamond in the secret compartment of your jewel case." She hesitated. "He might— well, he might be lurking around, and he might get nasty. Especially, if he was the one who dropped it in the cottage."

"Well, for heaven's sake," Honey exploded. "That's exactly what I said to you this morning when you dashed off through the poison ivy after him. You weren't afraid then."

"As usual," Trixie said ruefully, "I didn't stop to

think. But I have been thinking about it lots since. I'm not afraid for myself, because I haven't got the diamond. But I *am* afraid for you, Honey. You've just got to be awfully careful until we solve this mystery."

Chapter 4
Telltale Footprints

Honey shuddered. "We're not even going to try to solve this mystery, Trixie Belden," she said firmly. "If you, of all people, are scared, I'm going right back to the house and tell Jim everything."

"I'm not scared," Trixie said, frowning. "And you have no reason to worry unless you go wandering off at dusk by yourself. You're perfectly safe if you stay near the house. It's filled with people going in and out all day and most of the evening. Come on. Let's get the tools."

For answer, Honey turned around and started back up the lawn toward her house. "Neither of us is going down there," she said, squaring her shoulders. "That cottage is too near the woods, and it's getting dark and shadowy now."

"But how about the pruning saws and the shovels?" Trixie asked. "I'll dash down and get them so Miss Trask won't be too angry with us."

"Take one step and I'll scream," Honey said. "I mean it, Trixie. You may think I'm in danger, but so are you. Oh, I wish we'd never gone inside that horrid place and found that horrid diamond."

"Oh, all right," Trixie said reluctantly. "We can get the stuff early tomorrow morning and bring it back to the tool house before Gallagher drives out from the village."

"*If* he shows up," Honey said. "Oh, dear, if he's really quit, Miss Trask will want to know why, and then I'll have to tell her everything."

"You won't have to tell her *every*thing," Trixie argued. "Please, please, Honey, let's keep the diamond a secret for a little while longer. If we search the cottage carefully tomorrow morning, we might find some clues."

"I'm never going to put my foot inside it again and neither are you," Honey said stubbornly.

Trixie laughed. "Let's be sensible, Honey. Let's say a tramp stole the diamond and spent last night in the cottage. The diamond slipped out of a hole in his pocket, and he didn't discover it was gone until he had traveled up the river for a few miles. When he came back to look for it, we were there, and he heard us talking about it. So now he knows we have it. He certainly isn't going to keep on looking for it in the cottage."

"I guess not," Honey admitted. "What will he do?"

"My guess," Trixie said, "is that he lurked around

in the woods all day trying to figure out a way of getting into your house without being seen. He must realize by now that *that* is hopeless. So I think he may spend the night in the cottage and then go on his way north." She shrugged. "What else can he do?"

"Nothing," Honey said. "He can't very well come up to the house and knock on the door and demand that I give him something he stole."

"That's right," Trixie said. "He's probably more afraid of us than we are of him. For all he knows, we may have turned the diamond over to the police by now. In fact," she finished, "he must be afraid of that. He's probably already gone and is miles away."

Honey sighed. "Then why did you scare me half to death a few minutes ago?"

"Because," Trixie said, "I hadn't thought it through. Ever since lunch I've been trying to remember what we said after I first got the feeling that someone was watching us from the thicket. While we were grooming the horses, I finally remembered that it was after that when you told me where you had put the diamond. I got to worrying about you and stopped thinking." She giggled. "I can't seem to do two things at once. When I started to think again, I stopped worrying. Right now I'm not thinking, because I *know* I'm going to get an awful bawling out when I get home. Good night." She scampered off down the path to the hollow.

Trixie did receive a severe scolding when she arrived. "But, Moms," she wailed, "vacation is almost over. Soon I'll have to be in *bed* at nine. Can't we change the rule so I can stay up at Honey's later until school starts?"

"If you'd only phoned for permission," Mrs. Belden said, shaking her head. "When you weren't here at nine-fifteen your father called the Manor House, but the line was busy. I finally got so worried we called information and got the number of Regan's room. He reported that you were on your way home."

"I should have called," Trixie admitted. "And I'm very sorry." She grinned hopefully. "I haven't got any excuse except the old one. I didn't think."

Mr. Belden smiled. "Honesty deserves some reward, I guess. We'll let you off this once. And when Brian and Mart come back, we will extend the rule to nine-thirty until school opens. As long as you're with them, your mother won't worry."

"Gee, thanks, Dad," Trixie said, and hurried up to her room.

The next morning, when she and Bobby climbed the hill to the Manor House, they saw that the old, dark-green car was again parked in front of the garage. Regan introduced them to the new chauffeur.

"Dick," he said, "this is Trixie Belden and her kid brother, Bobby. They live in the little white farmhouse down in the hollow."

The tall, blond man bowed. "How do you do, Miss Trixie and Master Bobby."

Trixie shook hands with him and said, "Please don't call me 'miss,' Dick. I'm just plain Trixie."

"Hey," Bobby interrupted. "You're a chowpur, Dick. What's a chowpur?"

Dick grinned down at him. "It means I drive cars and take care of their motors. When your legs get a little longer, I'll teach you how to shift gears."

"Yippee!" Bobby yelled with delight. "An' I'll teach you how to catch frogs in Mummy's best strainer."

"So," Trixie scolded. "That's where it disappeared! You're a bad boy, Bobby Belden! Moms looked all over the place for that big strainer yesterday."

"Ah, don't scold the kid." Dick reached into his pocket and produced two quarters. "Here, Bobby. You can buy yourself a strainer for your very own."

Bobby stared with his round, blue eyes at the money which Dick dropped into his fat little hand. "For my very own," he repeated. "Hey! For my very own!"

Just then Miss Trask appeared. "I gave Mr. Wheeler your letter of recommendation," she told Dick. "He's leaving on a business trip with Mrs. Wheeler in about an hour and said to tell you to start work today if you like."

"I'd like to very much," Dick said. "I'm to sleep in, I suppose?"

Miss Trask nodded. "There's another bedroom over the garage. You and Regan can share the same living-room and bath in the suite."

Dick scowled. "Over the garage? I took it for granted that I'd sleep in the house."

Miss Trask looked surprised, but she said cheerfully, "Oh, you'll like sharing Regan's suite much better. The rooms are very comfortable and attractive. There's a television set and a fine radio-phonograph and a private telephone which you are at liberty to use for all the private calls you wish to make."

"You couldn't pay me to sleep in the house," Regan said, reaching into the back of Dick's car for his suitcase. "Come on, fella, I'll help you put your gear away."

"Gimme that!" It was almost a snarl, and Trixie stared at the new chauffeur who grabbed his bag roughly away from Regan.

Regan stared at him, too. "Take it easy, fella," he

said quietly. "I only meant to be helpful."

Instantly the expression on Dick's face changed. "Sorry," he said contritely. "Got two new summer uniforms in my grip and a bottle of black shoe polish. If it broke, I'd be out fifty bucks!"

"Fifty dollars," Miss Trask said, scribbling on a pad. "You'll be reimbursed at once, Richard. Mr. Wheeler said you were to charge anything you needed at the Sleepyside Department Store."

"Thanks," Dick said pleasantly. "I thought I might as well come prepared, so I bought a couple of gabardine coats and caps yesterday in town."

"Fine." Miss Trask smiled at him. "As soon as you're settled a bit, you'd better get into uniform. Mr. and Mrs. Wheeler will want you to drive them to the station. They're taking the eleven forty-seven express to New York." She hurried away into the house.

Trixie followed her more slowly. Bobby flatly refused to leave his new friend, and with an important air, led the way up the stairs to the suite over the garage.

In the spacious hall of the Manor House, Trixie met Honey.

"Such excitement," Honey said wearily. "Every time Daddy tries to take a vacation, something happens. When Mother heard he had to go to Chicago this morning, she didn't know whether to go with him or not."

"I take it she's going," Trixie said. "But I know she hated to leave you, Honey."

Honey nodded. "I could have gone along, but they won't be back for at least a week." She slipped her arm through Trixie's. "I couldn't be gone that long; not with what's upstairs in my jewelry box. Let's search the cottage for more clues."

As they strolled down the lawn, Trixie asked, "Are we in the doghouse? Did Gallagher really quit?"

"That's right," Honey said, "but Miss Trask isn't angry with us. She's already hired another gardener. A man named Nailor appeared right after breakfast asking for the job. He didn't have any really good references, but Daddy said to try him out for a week. Nobody could be worse than Gallagher was." She giggled. "I dashed right down to the cottage and brought the pruning saws and shovels back to the tool house. And I do mean dash. I was scared to death for fear someone was lurking in the woods."

"I'm sorry I said what I did yesterday," Trixie admitted. "Whoever was eavesdropping must be miles away by now. I hope you didn't take the flashlights back to the tack room," she added. "I think we ought to go over every inch of the floor. Maybe we'll find more footprints."

"I never even thought about the flashlights," Honey said. "Here they are. Right where we left them, outside by the window."

"Thank goodness it didn't rain last night," Trixie said. "The batteries would have been ruined and Regan would have been as mad as anything."

Honey smiled. "We get worse every day, you and I. We're always taking things and forgetting to return them."

Inside the cottage, they got down on their hands and knees with the flashlights and examined the dirt floor.

"This looks like another footprint," Trixie said suddenly. "And it's not the same as the other one. Look, it was made by a rubber heel. You can see the trade-mark plainly."

Honey pointed the beam of her torch on the new clue. "You're absolutely right, Trixie. Two men must have been in here since the rain Monday night. And they must have walked up and down a lot. That's why we can't find the other footprints. They've been scuffed away."

Trixie thought for a minute. "I don't think they walked up and down. I think they had a fight. That's why all but the two heelmarks were scuffed away."

"Oh, oh," Honey gasped. "They fought over the diamond, Trixie. Maybe one of them murdered the other one!" She moved closer to Trixie. "Now I *am* scared!"

Trixie grinned. "You're as bad as I am, Honey. You're letting your imagination run away with you. People don't go around killing other people for a diamond which they go off and leave behind."

Honey sighed with relief. Then she frowned with a puzzled expression on her pretty face. "Why *did* they go off and leave the diamond behind, Trixie? It's very, very valuable."

Trixie shrugged. "One of them dropped it while they were fighting, and it got ground into the mud. Then maybe they heard someone coming and hid in the woods. When they came back, we had already taken the diamond away."

Honey shuddered. "Maybe two men were hiding in the thicket yesterday. Maybe both of them know I have the diamond. Oh, Trixie, I can't stand it."

Trixie went outside and stared into the thicket. "No poison ivy in there," she said. "The wild honeysuckle must have choked it all out. Let's go in and see if we can find any more clues." She pulled away some of the vines and pushed her way through others. Then she stopped, staring at the ground. "The man with rubber heels was hiding here yesterday, Honey. Look."

Honey peered over her shoulder at the footprints. "You're right, Trixie," she said. "The trade-mark is the same. What happened to the man with the leather heels?"

Trixie pushed clear through the thicket to the path in the woods. She followed it down to Glen Road, with Honey right behind her.

"You're wasting your time looking for clues in the woods," Honey said. "There are too many pine needles."

Trixie stopped short so suddenly that Honey almost banged into her. "Look," she said, pointing. "Tire marks and more footprints! *Both* kinds of footprints!"

Chapter 5
Bobby's Secrets

Sure enough, on the soft shoulder of the road, there were unmistakable signs that a car had been parked there since the Monday night rain and that two men had walked from it toward the cottage.

Honey giggled nervously. "We're as smart as real detectives, Trixie. Two men, who have a car, must have spent Tuesday night in the cottage."

Trixie nodded. She walked north along the road a yard or so and then stopped. "Here are more tire marks but only rubber-heeled footprints."

Honey joined her. "What do you deduce, Sherlock?"

Trixie grinned. "I deduce that Mr. Rubber Heels came back later and parked the car at this spot. But Mr. Leather Heels wasn't with him, or else he stayed in the car."

"Or else he has wings," Honey agreed, "or seven-league boots. If he walked anywhere along the shoulder, he would have left footprints."

"Mr. Rubber Heels," Trixie said thoughtfully, "walked straight into the woods from the car. Then he came out of the woods and got into his car. The way the footprints point shows that."

"They certainly do," Honey said. "I'll tell you what I think happened. Gallagher mowed the lawns early Wednesday morning. The men saw him and were afraid he might come into the cottage. So they drove away in such a hurry they didn't realize one of them had dropped the diamond."

"That's what I think," Trixie said. "Later they drove back and parked here. Mr. Leather Heels stayed in the car, and Mr. Rubber Heels sneaked through the woods to make sure the coast was clear before he dared search the cottage. When he arrived, we were cutting away the vines from the window, so he hid in the thicket. When he heard the dogs barking, he hurried back to the car and they both drove away."

Honey laughed. "Thank goodness, the mystery is solved. When we turn the diamond over to the police, all they'll have to look for is a man with rubber heels who also has a bad case of poison ivy. When the detectives see these tire tracks, they can probably tell what kind of car to look for." She turned around. "I've got to dash back to the house and say good-by to Mother and Daddy. If I hurry, there'll just be time for Daddy to call the Sleepyside police station and—"

Trixie grabbed her arm. "Don't you dare tell your father anything, Honey Wheeler. If you do, we'll probably both end up in jail."

Honey gasped. "Wh-what on earth for?"

Trixie shook her head sadly. "Don't you realize that the men who stole the diamond and dropped it in the cottage must be in another state by now? They may never be caught, all because we didn't turn the diamond over to the police the minute we found it. It's all my fault," she admitted ruefully. "And there's some awful law about withholding information which might lead to the capture of criminals."

Honey gasped again. "Well, let's not withhold it another minute!"

"Please," Trixie begged. "Listen a minute, Honey. I think we may be able to capture the criminals ourselves. Then nobody'll be mad at us for keeping the diamond a secret."

"I think you're crazy," Honey said, pulling away from her. "You just said the police might not be able to catch the diamond thieves. What makes you think we can?"

"If you'd only listen," Trixie moaned. "I think the two men will come back later on. But they won't if there's even a suspicion that police are on their trail. As long as they feel sure they have only you and me to worry about, they may try to get it from us. We'll set some sort of trap and they'll walk right into it." She tightened her grip on Honey's slender arm. "Then we'll be heroines." She lowered her voice to a whisper. "That new gardener of yours who hasn't got very good references—he may be one of the gang."

Honey's hazel eyes were wide with admiration. "How smart you are, Trixie! I didn't like his looks at all. He's sort of shriveled and bent and, well—he made me think of a giant peanut, with no eyes to speak of."

"Is he going to sleep in?" Trixie asked.

Honey nodded. "He arrived C.O.D. in a taxi and said he wouldn't take the job unless he could sleep in. There are only three bedrooms on the third floor, you know. The cook and Celia have two of them, so Miss Trask had to plead with Regan to let the new chauffeur share his suite over the garage." She sighed. "You're *so* right about the servant problem, Trixie. Regan didn't like the idea at all at first. Although he never uses the other bedroom, he *has* got lots of his personal belongings in the living-room. You know, pictures and books and such."

Trixie laughed. "I'll bet Miss Trask won him over to the idea of sharing the suite with Dick pretty quickly.

Regan has wanted your family to hire a chauffeur ever since you moved up here." She sobered. "What's the new gardener's name?"

"Nailor," Honey told her. "Oh, oh, Trixie. He may have already taken the diamond from my jewel box!"

"Not a chance," Trixie said. "Not in the daytime. Your house is always crawling with people. He wouldn't even dare spy around. But tonight—tonight—"

Just then a gleaming midnight-blue sedan turned out of the Wheelers' driveway and headed up the road toward them.

"It's Mother and Daddy on the way to the station," Honey cried. "I've got to stop them and say good-by." She waved her arms frantically, and the car slowed to a stop.

Trixie watched while Honey climbed in to kiss her parents, and then both girls waved until the car disappeared from view.

"Our new chauffeur is certainly handsome in his uniform," Honey said. "What a difference! Regan couldn't be made to wear one. Not that anybody cared."

"Speaking of Regan," Trixie said, "reminds me of Bobby. I'd better go see what he's up to." They hurried along the road and up the steep driveway. At the top, they could see that Jim was giving Bobby a riding lesson in the corral. "Moms," Trixie panted, "would give me the dickens if she knew what a nuisance Bobby is to all of you. I'm forever leaving him with Jim or Regan when it's really my job to look out for him."

"Don't let it worry you," Honey said, stopping to catch her breath by a clump of rhododendron. "They both adore the little imp. We all do." She put out her hand to hold Trixie back. "You were saying something about the gardener which gave me goose pimples. Do you really think that Nailor is a—"

"That must be he now," Trixie interrupted as a wizened little man appeared in the hollyhock bed by the stable. "He looks more like a monkey than a peanut."

Honey smiled. "We don't see eye-to-eye on anything. You thought our new chauffeur, Dick, looked like a weasel, and I think he's very nice-looking."

"I still think he looks like a weasel," Trixie insisted. "His eyes are close together." She grinned. "Maybe I should have said mink, because he did look super in his uniform—and, he *was* awfully nice with Bobby when they met. He gave him fifty cents, so he could catch frogs in his own strainer."

Honey pushed her bangs away from her perspiring forehead. "I'm getting confused—weasels, minks, and frogs. As Regan would say, what next?"

"The next *step*," Trixie said, "is for you to invite me to spend the night with you."

"But that's a standing invitation," Honey said, chuckling. "You know that, Trixie."

"Thanks," Trixie said. "I accept. But Miss Trask had better let Moms know she really wants me. Bobby and I seem to live here."

"You and Bobby," Honey cried impulsively, "are the nicest things that ever happened to me—except for Jim. And, if it hadn't been for you, I would never have had him for a brother. Oh, please, Trixie," she finished. "Let me tell him about the diamond."

Trixie sniffed. "And have him make fun of our theories? Or, worse still, report us to the FBI? You know perfectly well, Honey Wheeler, this is no time to let Jim in on the secret. Later," she added mysteriously, "we may need his help."

While Trixie was helping her mother fix luncheon, Miss Trask called, inviting Trixie for supper and to spend the night. When Mrs. Belden came back from the phone, she said, "They're so hospitable, Trixie, I never can say no. Are you sure you're not wearing out your welcome?"

Trixie grinned. "They've already put an extra leaf

in the dining-room table so there'll be room for Brian and Mart. And they fixed up the extra guest rooms for them, too." She hugged her mother impulsively. "I really like our house much better than any place in the world, but it is fun to go visiting."

"Of course it is." Mrs. Belden smiled. "And I don't suppose you have tomatoes almost every meal the way we do down here when they're in season."

"Only because Gallagher was such a lazy gardener," Trixie said. "They have even more tomatoes than we have, but nobody picks them except Miss Trask, and she's almost always too busy to go near the vegetable garden."

"What a pity," Mrs. Belden said as she dried tender baby lettuce leaves in a clean dish towel. "Maybe a nice way for you to repay them for their hospitality would be for you to take them some of my homemade tomato juice."

"They'd love it," Trixie said. "But they'd like your green tomato chutney the best of all, Moms. You can't buy anything like that in the stores."

"Fine," Mrs. Belden said. "Remind me when I start picking the green tomatoes early in October." She laughed. "I mean, when *you* pick them for me."

"It never seems to end," Trixie said with a moan.

"Sometimes, Moms, I wish you hadn't been born with a green thumb."

"Speaking of which," her mother said, "there are beans to be picked and early potatoes to be dug. And don't go up to Honey's this afternoon until you've gathered the eggs and fed the chickens."

It was after six when Trixie climbed the hill to the Manor House, and she was so tired from working in the garden she knew she would fall asleep the minute she got into Honey's big bed.

"But I've *got* to stay awake," she wailed inwardly. "I just know Nailor will try to sneak into Honey's room and get the diamond." She stopped, suddenly, as she heard stealthy footsteps on the path behind her. She wheeled. "Bobby Belden, what do you mean by following me with that jar full of leopard frogs? Go and put them right back in the pond."

"Won't," Bobby said firmly. "I'm gonna show 'em to Dickie. Mummy said I could."

"Are you sure she said you could?" Trixie demanded suspiciously. "It's your suppertime."

Bobby nodded until his blond curls danced. "Sure as sure. Hey! I love Dickie and he loves me." He trotted along beside Trixie, clutching the jar of frogs.

Trixie made sure that there were enough air holes

punched in the metal top. "I wish you'd stop catching frogs," she said. "It's sort of cruel. Even though you do let them go right afterward."

"Is not cruel," Bobby said. "They like it. I feed 'em flies and things. I love frogs 'most as much as I love Reddy and Patch and Regan and Dickie. But Dickie," he confided in a lower tone of voice, "is 'fraid of horses."

"I don't believe it," Trixie said with a sniff.

"He is so," Bobby insisted. "Tol' me so his very own self. But he loves Patch and Reddy. Bought 'em some big bones when he droved into the village. Oh, oh," he finished. "That was see-crud."

"Don't be silly," Trixie said. "Why should it be a secret? It was very nice of him to bring some bones back to the dogs."

"We have lots of see-cruds," Bobby said smugly. "I showed Dickie all round Honey's place today. I showed him the wading pool and the cottage and Honey's windows. That's a see-crud, too."

"Well, I'm glad you had fun," Trixie said absentmindedly, and added to herself, *Bobby and his secrets! He's hopeless!*

The plump little boy raced ahead of her to show his prizes to the new chauffeur, tripped on an exposed tree root, and fell on the rocky path. The jar broke with a loud crash. For a moment, Trixie was too frightened to move. Broken glass was all around him—was Bobby badly cut?

He was yelling as though he were suffering from a million serious wounds, and Trixie forced her trembling legs to carry her to his side. But Dick reached the child first and lifted him up in his arms.

"There, there, Bobby," he said, in a reassuring voice. "You haven't got a scratch."

Trixie saw, with relief, that Bobby was only screaming because his leopard frogs were hopping off into the ferns as fast as they could. The new chauffeur gave her a disapproving glance. "You ought to have better sense," he muttered. "The idea of letting a little boy run around with a jar in his arms!"

"My frogs," Bobby shrieked. "I've losted 'em all!"

"Never mind," Dick said, setting the boy down on the ground. "I'll help you catch some more." To Trixie, he added in a disagreeable tone of voice, "You'd better get a broom and clean up that broken glass."

"It wasn't my fault," Trixie retorted. "But I'll clean it up. Thanks," she added sarcastically, "for offering to help."

A dark flush spread over his pale features. "I haven't time," he told her coldly. "And it *was* your fault.

You're supposed to take care of that kid, and you go off and leave him for hours at a time."

It was Trixie's turn to flush. She squared her shoulders. "I'm sorry Bobby took up so much of your valuable time this afternoon. It won't happen again." And she marched off to the stable for a broom and trash can.

He stood watching her, insolently grinning, while she swept and picked up the broken pieces of glass. When she finished, he said, "Let that be a lesson to you. Palling around with a rich little girl has sort of made you forget that you're supposed to work for the money your dad gives you every week, hasn't it?"

Trixie ignored him. She started Bobby off on the path that led down to their home and said, "Go right into the house. Your supper is waiting for you."

"I won't go home by my own self," he yelled. "Hey! I want Dickie to take me home."

Dick immediately took the boy's fat little hand. "Sure, I'd be glad to, Bobby," he said affably.

Trixie, her hands on her hips, watched them stroll down the hill. "Well, I never," she cried exasperatedly. "He's too busy to help me pick up the pieces, but he's Bobby's willing slave."

Down in the hollow, they were joined by the two dogs. Reddy and Patch greeted the new chauffeur affectionately, and that made Trixie crosser than ever. "This must be Dick's 'Be kind to children and animals week,' " she reflected bitterly. "Anybody over twelve is beneath his notice."

"Talking to yourself?"

Trixie whirled around to face Jim who must have come quietly down from the back of the house. "No," she told him. "I'm simply boiling over. That new chauffeur is as mean as a snake." She explained, but instead of being sympathetic, Jim merely chuckled.

"You can't expect everyone who works around here to be the good sport Regan is," he said. "Regan is something pretty special. I'll bet there's not another groom in the world who would put up with what he puts up with, and no complaints." He picked up the trash can and broom. "I'll put these away for you. Honey's on the front porch champing at the bit because you didn't show up when you said you would."

"Thanks a lot, Jim," Trixie said, and added gratefully, "You and Regan are both swell to help me take care of Bobby. I'll try to be better after this."

Inwardly, she was thinking, *Bobby must have given Dick a play-by-play description of what the Belden family does every day. How else could he have known that Dad gives me five dollars a week for helping Moms?*

As she walked along the graveled driveway, she tried to remember what Bobby had said to her about the secrets he shared with the new chauffeur. Something he had said didn't make sense. If Dick were very modest, he might not want it known that he had bought some bones in the village for the dogs. That would explain that "see-crud." But what else was it Bobby had told her?

Then Trixie remembered. "I showed Dickie all round Honey's place today," Bobby had said smugly. "I showed him the wading pool and the cottage and Honey's windows. That's a see-crud, too."

Honey's windows! That was it, and now it did make sense!

Chapter 6
Midnight Prowler

Dinner at the Manor House was usually such a formal affair that it never failed to awe Trixie. She was always terrified of using the wrong fork or spoon; and, no matter how careful she was, she always managed to spill something on the snowy white tablecloth.

But on Thursdays, the cook's night off, the meal was a much more simple affair. Celia served the first course, and then she and Miss Trask brought in platters of cold cuts and big bowls of salad. Everyone helped himself, and the dessert was usually fruit and crackers with several kinds of cheese. Grownups were served coffee in fragile little cups.

This Thursday night, Trixie made up her mind that she would have some coffee, too. Otherwise, she would never stay awake. And she *had* to stay awake. Someone, she was sure, would sneak into Honey's room after everyone else was asleep—someone who knew that there was a valuable diamond in the secret compartment of her jewelry box. That someone might turn out to be the new gardener, Nailor—or the new chauffeur, Dick.

73

When Celia brought in Miss Trask's coffee, Trixie pushed back her chair and jumped to her feet. She grabbed the nearest platter and said, "I'll help you clear the table, Celia. I always do it at home." She pushed through the swinging door into the butler's pantry. On the drain board was a large cup of black coffee which Celia had obviously just poured for herself. Trixie slid the platter of cold cuts in between the pots and pans beside the sink, and grabbed the cup.

After the first swallow, she almost screamed with pain. It was scalding hot and as strong as lye. Trixie had never tasted coffee before. It was horrible, but she forced herself to gulp down as much as her protesting throat would let her, and hurried back into the dining-room.

"Why, Trixie," Honey gasped. "You've been crying. What's the matter?"

Trixie hastily dabbed at her watering eyes with her napkin.

"Oh, dear," Miss Trask said worriedly. "Don't tell me you're a hay fever victim, Trixie? This is the ragweed season, you know."

Celia sniffed. "More likely, onions is the answer. Trixie loves onions, and I left some thick slices in the pantry. I forgot Mr. Wheeler wouldn't be here for supper. He loves 'em, too."

Jim laughed. "You'd better snitch a slice, too, Honey. Otherwise, Trixie's breath will drive you crazy all night."

"Radishes are worse," Honey said, nibbling one. "Anyway, the bologna was laced with garlic. We're all in the same boat, or breath, I guess."

Later, when the girls were upstairs in Honey's room getting ready for bed, she said, "You were crying, Trixie. That's why you hurried out to the butler's pantry. And I know why." She gave Trixie an impulsive hug. "Jim told me that Dick was rude to you. I'm perfectly furious. If Daddy were here, I'd see to it that he was fired tomorrow. He said something that hurt your feelings, didn't he?"

Trixie hesitated. She wanted to share her suspicions of the new chauffeur with her best friend. She longed to blurt out, "He found out from Bobby which windows on this floor are yours. So now he knows where your bedroom is. He may sneak in here tonight and try to get the diamond. I think he's one of the two men who left it in the cottage."

But suppose she was wrong in her suspicions? Bobby loved to give out information of any kind. It made him feel important. He might well, without any coaxing, have told his new friend where every member of the Wheeler household slept.

Trixie quickly decided that there was no sense in worrying Honey until she could prove her suspicions. And tonight she should be able to prove them. So she merely tossed her short, blond curls and said, "Pooh. That skinny, little weasel couldn't hurt my feelings." She quickly changed the subject. "A fine hostess you are! Why don't you help me unpack my overnight kit?"

Honey collapsed on the big bed, shaking with laughter. Trixie's overnight kit consisted of a tooth-brush hastily wrapped in a clean handkerchief. She always borrowed pajamas from Honey when she spent the night at the Manor House.

Honey, still giggling, handed her a pair now. "There," she said. "Don't you dare say I'm not a good hostess. What else does your royal highness wish?"

"Soap, towel, and washcloth, please," Trixie said airily. "I'm going to take a cold shower."

"A cold shower?" Honey stared at her. "Why, it'll keep you awake, Trixie, and you told me yourself that you had to get up at the crack of dawn to feed the chickens."

"Nothing could keep me awake," Trixie said. "I'm so tired I can hardly keep my eyes open."

The cold shower did make her more wide-awake for a short while, but, in spite of the fact that she had gulped down half a cup of strong, black coffee, Trixie fell asleep before it was quite dark outside.

When she awoke, it was pitch black and stiflingly hot. Someone was stealthily opening the door to Honey's room. Trixie felt the sound more than she heard it, and, still groggy with sleep and weariness, she yelled at the top of her lungs.

"Who's there?"

Too late, she remembered that she had planned to catch one of the two new employees with his hand on Honey's jewelry box. She scrambled out of bed and dashed to the door. Honey was mumbling something in a frightened, bewildered voice, but Trixie didn't pay any attention. Someone had just darted around the corner of the long, carpeted hall. She tore after him and collided with Jim when he burst out of his room. Miss Trask appeared, then, too, her crisp gray hair rumpled, her bright blue eyes blinking in the light of the hall.

"Who yelled?" Jim demanded.

"Me," Trixie said. "I had a nightmare, I guess."

Honey joined them, then. "Wh-what on earth happened?" she asked. "Something woke me up, and then I saw Trixie dashing out of the room."

Trixie forced herself to smile. If only she hadn't yelled! She might have caught the person who was probably at this very moment tiptoeing down the back

77

stairs—or tiptoeing *up* them to his room on the third floor. "I had a nightmare," she said again. "I'm sorry I woke you."

Honey laughed. "It was that cold shower, Trixie. I warned you."

"Well, go back to bed, all of you," Miss Trask said. "It's midnight."

The big grandfather clock in the downstairs hall was striking when the girls climbed back into Honey's big bed. Honey fell asleep on the eleventh stroke, but Trixie lay awake for a long time, thinking.

Why hadn't she told Jim and Miss Trask the truth? If she had, Jim would probably have caught the prowler before he got away. Who was the prowler? The new chauffeur or the new gardener? It would have been easy for Nailor, if he knew that Honey had the diamond, to sneak down from his room on the floor above. And it would have been almost as easy for Dick to sneak into the house through the kitchen door. Trixie knew that when Miss Trask closed up the house on hot nights, she simply hooked the flimsy latches on the screen doors. Anyone could lift those latches from the outside by slipping a knife through the crack.

Suddenly, Trixie couldn't stand it another minute. She had to know whether or not the kitchen door was latched. If it was, the midnight prowler must have been Nailor. If the latch was not in place, then the man she had frightened away must be Dick.

She slipped out of Honey's room and tiptoed down the hall to the back stairs. They were only dimly lighted and she had to grope her way down, clinging to the railing. It was not a pleasant feeling. Suppose the midnight prowler was lurking in the shadows of the hall below?

At the bottom, Trixie took a deep breath and dashed across the dark hall and through the swinging door into the kitchen. She knew that Miss Trask always left a light burning above the sink, but it was not turned on now. The door swung to behind her, leaving her in complete darkness.

A thick wall of blackness surrounded her on all sides, and Trixie felt as though she couldn't breathe. She wanted to turn around and race back to Honey's room, but she couldn't move. She could only stand there, listening, for someone was coming quietly down the back stairs. Whoever it was, was not groping, so he must be carrying a flashlight. Now he was crossing the hall. Now he was pushing open the swinging door. The beam of a flashlight cut through the darkness, and Trixie whirled around, stifling a scream.

It was Jim.

"Say, what goes on?" he demanded in a loud whisper. "You're up to something, Trixie. I didn't fall for that nightmare yarn of yours." He grabbed her arm. "What cooks?"

Trixie let out her pent-up breath. She felt like laughing and crying, but she didn't dare do either. She didn't dare make any noise at all. Miss Trask might wake up and hear them.

"I'll explain everything in the morning, Jim," she whispered. "Honest, I will."

"It had better be good," he hissed and held the door open for her.

Trixie meekly climbed up the stairs ahead of him. They separated outside Honey's room, and Trixie crept silently into bed.

The next morning she dressed while Honey was still sleeping and hurried out of the house. She was starting down the path to the hollow when Jim hailed her from his bedroom window.

"Wait for me," he said. "I'll help you feed the chickens. They may need fresh water."

In a few minutes he joined her, wearing swimming trunks. As they walked down the path together, Trixie told him how she and Honey had found the diamond in the old cottage and why she suspected one of the two new employees.

80

"You girls are the limit," he groaned. "You should have turned that diamond right over to Dad."

"I know," Trixie admitted. She scattered grain in front of the chicken coop. "The mash hoppers are almost empty, Jim. You fill them, please."

"I will," he said, "but don't try to change the subject. You're insane to suspect Dick, Trixie. I happen to know that the last man he worked for is a very good friend of Dad's. Dad showed me that letter of recommendation. And as for Nailor, he's not what you'd call a landscape gardener, but he *has* lived in Sleepyside all his life and has a very good reputation. He has clipped the hedges and tended the flowers of leading citizens for years."

But Trixie wasn't listening. She was staring, open-mouthed, at the back terrace of her house. Two tall, tanned boys were standing by the kitchen door.

"Brian," she yelled. "Mart! Jim, look. They're home from camp already."

Trixie's brothers jumped over the low stone wall of the terrace to meet her as she raced toward them. After she had hugged them both, she dragged them to the chicken coop where Jim was waiting to be introduced.

Brian shook hands with him and said, "Gee, it's great news that you live up in the Manor House. Trixie wrote us about you and Honey."

"Scribbled is the word, Jim," Mart said with a grin. "It took us hours to decipher her message, but when we did, we decided we were missing too much fun at home. So here we are."

"But your jobs," Trixie said. "I thought camp didn't close until tomorrow."

"It doesn't," Brian told her. "But the nursery group left yesterday afternoon. With the small fry gone, there wasn't anything for us to do but pack up the things they left behind." He sighed. "Our little charges were all about Bobby's age, so you can imagine the junk they collected."

"By the time we finished cleaning the cabins," Mart added, "we decided that we'd never be junior counselors again. Our boss took pity on us; and, since he had to drive through Sleepyside on his way home, he dropped us off here last night."

"Boy, am I ever glad to see you two," Jim said enthusiastically. "Maybe you can talk your wacky sister into turning the diamond she and Honey found over to the police."

"Wacky, yes," blond Mart jeered, "but the finder of diamonds, no. When her imagination gets going, a piece of coal becomes a priceless ruby overnight."

"Truer words were never spoken," Brian agreed.

"When you've known Trixie as long as we have, Jim, you'll stop listening to her tall tales."

"I'm beginning to catch on," Jim said, grinning. "Last night she heard a mysterious prowler, whom nobody else heard, and she suspects our new chauffeur and gardener."

"A man or a mouse," Mart said, shaking his head, "it makes no diff to Trixie. They're all crooks if they so much as poke their noses out of their lairs after dark."

"Is that so?" Trixie demanded. "Mice don't live in lairs, smarty. We did so find a valuable diamond. Wait until you see it."

Just then Honey appeared at the top of the path. "Trixie! Jim!" she yelled as she raced down the hill. When she caught sight of Brian and Mart she skidded to a stop and added shyly, "Oh, your brothers came home from camp sooner than they expected."

"That's right," Trixie said. "The one on my left with the funny-looking crew cut is Mart. The other odd-looking creature is Brian. I hate them both at the moment. They don't believe we found a real diamond, Honey."

Honey shook hands with the boys, smiling. "But it is a real diamond," she told them. "You can see for yourselves. I brought it with me." She reached into the pocket of her shorts and brought out the stone. The facets glittered in the early morning sunlight as she handed it to Brian.

"Holy cow," Mart gasped. "I asked for bread and she gave me cake. Where on earth did you find it?"

"That's not so important, now," Honey said soberly, "as where we're going to hide it. I don't dare keep it in my jewelry box any longer."

"Why not?" Trixie asked. "What's happened?"

"Nothing's happened," Honey said. "Not yet. But when I woke up this morning, I remembered what you'd said yesterday that gave me goose pimples. You said that Nailor might be one of the gang that stole the diamond. Why, Trixie, if he is, he could have sneaked into my room last night when we were asleep and taken it. The jewel box, I mean. If he knew the diamond was in it, it wouldn't take him long to find the secret compartment."

"Wait a minute, puh-leeze," Mart interrupted. "You're moving too fast for me. Let's start with where you found the diamond and then decide where we're going to hide it."

"Oh," Trixie cried excitedly, "then you don't think we ought to turn it over to the police?"

"Not me," Mart said, arching his sandy eyebrows. "If there's a mystery lying around loose waiting to be

solved, I want a crack at it before the experts take over."

"How about you, Brian?" Trixie asked her older brother.

"We-ell," he said thoughtfully. "When I know more about it, I might feel the way Mart does. We were going to have a swim before breakfast, but I guess that can wait." He stretched out in the long grass by the chicken coop. "Let's hear it, Trixie. And don't exaggerate any more than you have to."

Chapter 7
A Black Eye

Trixie perched on a big rock, and the others sprawled in the grass around it. She told the story from beginning to end.

"Oh, Trixie," Honey gasped. "Then Nailor did try to sneak into my room last night?"

"Nailor or Dick," Trixie said. "I frankly suspect Dick. Bobby told him which windows were yours."

"Are you sure you heard someone last night?" Jim asked. "Sure you weren't dreaming?"

"I'm positive," Trixie said. "When a door handle is turned it makes a special sort of grating sound. And when I dashed out into the hall I saw enough to be sure that someone had just disappeared around the corner where the back stairs are."

"What *did* you see?" Mart asked.

"I don't know how to explain it," Trixie admitted. "But there was *something* there, and half a second later, it wasn't. It might have been part of a man's jacket or bathrobe. But it was something, all right."

"Too bad you and Jim didn't check to see if the

was unlatched when you were in the kitchen
t," Brian said. "Now it's too late, I guess. Too
eople have already gone in and out of the house
by now."

"That's right," Jim said. "It would be hard to find
out who first opened the back door this morning, and
even if we did, he probably wouldn't remember whether
the latch was hooked or not." He turned to Trixie. "I'll go
along with you, although I don't suspect either Dick or
Nailor. Let's try to catch the prowler ourselves."

"Oh, wonderful," Trixie cried. "He should walk into
our trap tonight. If only I'd stayed awake last night,
we'd know now who he is."

"The first step," Jim said, "is for Honey to switch
rooms with me. You can be sure I won't yell if anyone
sneaks in. I'll keep a flashlight handy and catch him red-
handed."

"But suppose he has a gun?" Honey protested. "Oh,
Jim!"

"I'm not worried about that," Jim said. "If he had a
gun, he would have used it last night. What excuse can
we give Miss Trask for wanting to swap rooms?"

"I know," Trixie cried. "One of Honey's windows
faces east and the sun wakes her up at the crack of
dawn. That's why she wants to swap."

"Pretty flimsy, pretty flimsy," Brian said, "but if Miss Trask is the good sport you all say she is, you'll probably get by with it."

Honey nodded. "She's like Regan. Neither of them asks a lot of bothersome questions."

"They're both too busy minding their own business," Jim added.

"Dick," Trixie put in thoughtfully, "is supposed to be busy, too, but he spends a lot of time making friends with Bobby and the dogs. That's suspicious, if you ask me."

Jim frowned. "I'd agree with you if I hadn't seen the letter of recommendation from Mr. Whitney, who is one of Dad's best friends."

"And he's so very good-looking," Honey said. "Dick, I mean. People who steal diamonds and lurk around in thickets eavesdropping don't look like that."

Trixie sniffed. "How do you know they don't? Besides, Dick isn't nice-looking. He's mean. His lips are too thin, and his eyes are too close together."

Mart laughed. "You girls are wacky. Didn't you ever hear the old saying about not judging a book by its cover? Whether he's handsome or looks like Dracula has nothing to do with the case."

"Trixie's right about one thing," Jim said. "I guess I

should say *Bobby* is right. Dick *is* afraid of horses. When I came back from a ride on Jupe yesterday afternoon, Miss Trask called me in to the phone. I asked Dick to hold Jupe while I answered it, and he flatly refused. He said, 'You couldn't pay me to go near that rearing, prancing brute.' "

"He might have said that just because he doesn't do favors for anyone except Bobby," Trixie said. "Honestly, I was furious when he stood there grinning yesterday while I picked up the broken glass."

"That was horrid of him," Honey cried impulsively. "When Daddy hears about it, Dick will be fired."

"Don't be a tattletale on account of me," Trixie said. "Anyway, I don't think he'll be here when your father comes back."

"Why not?" Brian demanded.

"Because," Trixie said with a superior smile, "I'm sure he's our prowler. Jim will catch him tonight."

Brian shook his head. "A woman convinced against her will is of the same opinion still," he chanted. "Just because Bobby said he showed Dick Honey's windows doesn't mean a thing. Bobby's reports are generally garbled to death."

"That's not the only thing that makes me suspicious," Trixie said. "Come on, let's take a quick swim in the lake.

It must be almost time for breakfast." She started up the path and they all raced after her.

The girls were wearing denim shorts and halters so they didn't bother to change into swim suits. Honey had to stop long enough in the boathouse to get a cap to pull on over her shoulder-length bob. She was the last one in.

"Boy! Can she swim and dive," Mart whispered to Trixie as they lay on their backs, floating. "She could give us all lessons."

"Honey," Trixie said, "learned how to swim and ride at camps and boarding schools. She hardly knew her parents until this summer. That's why she had governesses. Miss Trask was the math instructor at the last school Honey went to. And," she added enviously, "Honey has already had some algebra. They taught it in the seventh grade. She'll probably get much better marks than I will."

"Oh, you'll be okay," Mart said affectionately. "It kills me to admit it, Trix, but you're really smart at times. What other reason makes you suspect Dick?"

"Let's go back to the boathouse and get dry in the sun," Trixie said. "I'll tell you, then."

When they were stretched out on the hot boards of the porch, she explained. "Dick was very disappointed when he heard he wasn't going to sleep in the house. He was mad when Miss Trask told him he was to share Regan's suite over the garage. He was so mad," she finished, "that he was rude to Regan. All Regan did was offer to help him carry up his suitcase, and Dick snarled and grabbed it away from him."

Mart rolled over on his stomach. "Aha, the plot thickens. Maybe there was a time bomb in his suitcase."

Trixie glanced at him swiftly and saw that he was laughing. "Oh, all right, make fun of me," she said crossly. "But I know Dick wanted to sleep in the house. That would have made it easier for him to swipe the diamond. This way, he has no excuse for ever going beyond the servants' dining-room next to the kitchen. But, if he had a room on the third floor, he—" She stopped, for Miss Trask was coming down the path to the lake.

"Good morning, Trixie," she said with a smile. "Your mother just phoned and told me your brothers came home last night. She wanted you to hurry home for breakfast, but I persuaded her to let you all have pancakes and sausages down here at the boathouse."

Mart and Trixie scrambled to their feet, and Trixie introduced him to Miss Trask. "Brian," she said, "is the tall, dark boy on the raft with Honey and Jim." She cupped her hands and yelled across the water. "*Brian!* Come back and meet Miss Trask. We're invited for breakfast."

Celia and one of the other maids brought trays of delicious food down to the boathouse, and in a few minutes they were all gathered around the rustic table on the sunny porch.

"This is the life," Mart said, buttering his fifth pancake. "At camp we were so busy seeing that our small fry didn't drown in the maple syrup, we didn't have time to eat ourselves."

"You look starved," Trixie said with a sniff. "You've both grown inches and gained tons."

"You haven't done so badly yourself," Brian said with a laugh. He turned to Jim. "Say, I think the boys' outdoor school you were telling me about is a great idea. Can I sign up now for the job of resident doctor?"

Jim nodded, grinning. "How about you, Mart? You like small fry. Will you be the kindergarten teacher at my school for underprivileged boys?"

"Thank you, no," Mart said with an elaborate bow. "One summer with that age group was enough for me. Next year I'm going to work on a farm. I plan to go to agricultural college when I get out of high school, you know."

"Swell," Jim said. "Part of the curriculum at my school will be farming. You can be in charge of that department."

"That, I accept," Mart said. "What about the girls? Trixie loves housework," he said sarcastically. "She'll be a big help. What she misses with a dust cloth would clog a vacuum hose."

"Is that so?" Trixie demanded. "I'll have you know that Honey and I did all the cooking on our trailer trip, and kept the *Swan* tidy, too."

"Well, *sort* of tidy," Honey said with a giggle. "Anyway, we're going to be detectives, Trixie and I."

Brian and Mart howled with laughter. "That does it," Brian said. "No matter what we do next summer, Mart, we'll have to take Trixie with us. Without us around, she goes completely off her rocker."

Trixie tossed her short, blond curls. "You and Jim," she told them, "are just too, too funny. Wait and see. We'll find out who dropped the diamond in the cottage long before you do."

"How do you know it was dropped?" Brian asked.

"Oh, for Pete's sake," Trixie gasped. "You don't think somebody deliberately buried it in the floor, do you? I got over the silly idea of looking for buried treasure in the cottage ages ago."

Honey told them then about the heelprints and the tire treadmarks they had found. "Trixie is really very smart about clues," she finished seriously.

"Let's all go have a look at those clues," Brian said. "But we'd better first change into shirts and dungarees on account of poison ivy."

"Once I go home, I'm stuck for hours," Trixie said mournfully. "There are about a thousand chores waiting for me. But Honey will show you what we found." She gathered up some of the dishes and led the way up the path.

After they had returned the trays to the kitchen, the Beldens cut across the driveway on their way home. Jim and Honey had stayed in the house to arrange with Miss Trask about swapping rooms for a while.

As Trixie passed the garage, she saw Dick lounging in the entrance. She stared at him with surprise. One of his eyes was black and blue and rapidly closing. His lips were puffy and sore-looking.

"What on earth happened to you?" she asked, without thinking. "Did you fall out of bed or something, Dick?"

"No, I didn't," he said sourly. "I was just trying to be helpful. Had a little extra time this morning, so I thought I'd give Regan a hand with the horses."

"How could you give him a hand?" Trixie demanded. "He left last night for his day off and won't be back until this evening."

"That's just what I mean," Dick snapped at her. "He's not here to groom the horses, so I thought I'd do them for him. The big black gelding kicked me. He ought to be shot."

Trixie could not suppress a laugh. "You should have better sense than to fool around with horses when you don't like them. Besides, Jupe didn't need a grooming. Jim rode him yesterday, and he never puts a horse away without brushing it and cleaning its hoofs and everything."

Brian nudged her. "You might introduce us, Sis."

"Oh," Trixie cried, embarrassed. "Dick, these are my brothers, Brian and Mart."

"Hi," the new chauffeur said coolly. "Hope you have better manners than your fresh sister."

Out of the corner of one eye, Trixie saw that Brian and Mart were furious; but they said nothing. Once they were out of earshot, however, Mart exploded. "Say, that guy has a nerve, calling you fresh, Trix. I've a good mind to take a poke at him."

"Trixie *was* fresh," Brian said easily. "But I'd just as soon black the guy's other eye for him."

"That's it," Trixie cried excitedly. "Dick was in a fight. Jupe never kicked him. If he had, the chauffeur would have a broken nose and no front teeth."

Mart nodded. "You've got something there, Trix. But who did the job on his face, do you suppose?"

"I can't imagine," Trixie said. "Regan has a red-hot temper, and I don't think he likes Dick much, but he left for his day off right after supper last night. Maybe the new gardener and Dick got into an argument."

"The one you said looks like a little monkey?" Brian asked. "If he blacked Dick's eye he must look more like a gorilla."

Trixie giggled. "You're right; Nailor couldn't possibly have beaten Dick up. He's so shriveled Honey thinks of him as a giant peanut. Nailor's even older than Gallagher, and he was positively ancient."

They had reached the chicken coop down in the hollow, and Trixie darted inside to see if there were any eggs. "Not a one," she said. "The hens are molting. And thank goodness, as of now, the chickens are your chore, Mart."

"Okay," he said cheerfully. "I like our feathered friends a lot better than I do the pre-school-agers. Gleeps, Trix! I must have made five million bread and butter and peanut butter sandwiches this summer."

"Speaking of which," Brian interrupted. "It's an old joke that when a boy comes home with a black eye, he always tells his father, 'You ought to see the other fellow.'

Maybe we ought to look around for the gardener's body."

"Nailor," Trixie said, "is very much alive. I saw him mowing the lawn down by the cottage a little while ago."

"There's another old joke," Mart said thoughtfully. "When a guy appears with a shiner, he's supposed to say he got it bumping into a door in the dark. How do you like that one, Trix?"

"I see what you mean," she said, narrowing her blue eyes. "Maybe Dick left the house in such a hurry last night that the swinging door to the kitchen gave him that black eye." She shuddered reminiscently. "It was pitch dark in there. Even if he didn't bang into the door, he might have stumbled over a chair and bruised his face against the sink."

"Wouldn't you have heard such a commotion?" Brian asked. "You or Jim or Miss Trask?"

"I doubt it," Trixie said. "We were all talking at once right after I dashed into the hall. And then the grandfather clock began to strike. It dongs and whirs and wheezes like anything, especially when it has the chore of telling the world that it's midnight."

"Let's not jump to conclusions," Brian said. "I don't like that Dick guy any more than you do, Trixie, even though his lips aren't too thin at the moment, and I can't tell with that shiner what his eyes normally are like. But who knows? He might have driven into town last night and got into a brawl at the dogwagon. That would explain why he lied and said that Jupiter kicked him."

"That's right," Mart agreed. "When the head of the house is away, even the most highly recommended chauffeur might take a little liberty here and there. Is there any law up at the Manor House, Trixie, that says the chauffeur has to stay in when Regan is off?"

"Oh, I don't think so," Trixie said. "Miss Trask may get around to that eventually, but they never had a chauffeur until yesterday when they hired Dick."

"And you found the diamond on Wednesday?" Brian shook his head. "It does seem like pretty much of a coincidence that both men applied for jobs so soon after that."

"I tell you what," Trixie interrupted as she was struck with an idea. "While I'm helping Moms, why don't you try to find out what kind of shoes Nailor and Dick wear? If their heels match the prints Honey and I found inside the cottage and by the road, we'll know that it wasn't a coincidence."

"Okay," Mart said, giving her a fond pat on the arm as he held the kitchen door open for her. "Get to your dusting, slave-girl. We vacationing men will take over the sleuthing!"

Chapter 8
Lost: A Diamond

Even though Trixie was busy every minute helping her mother, the morning dragged on and on. She kept wondering what the others were doing and if they had found any more clues.

Brian and Mart did not come back to the house until she was setting the table for lunch. Brian's face was expressionless, but Mart gave her a secret wink.

"Bobby," he said to his mother, as he scrubbed his hands at the kitchen sink, "is getting to be quite a horseman. Jim gave him a ride on Lady a while ago, and the kid's really good."

"Where is he now?" Mrs. Belden asked. "Didn't he come back from the Wheelers' with you?"

"Don't worry about him," Brian said easily. "When last seen he was helping, or rather, hindering, Jim and Honey who are swapping rooms. I'll run up and see if he's still under their feet."

"He probably invited himself to stay for lunch," Trixie said after Brian left. "Bobby is in full charge up there."

"We must be careful not to let him become a nuisance," Mrs. Belden said worriedly. "He could talk of no one but his new friend when I put him to bed last night—Dick. Is he the new gardener, Trixie?"

"No, Moms," Trixie said. "Dick's the new chauffeur." She crossed her fingers. "He and Bobby are just like this."

"Here they come now," Mart said from the window that looked out on the back terrace. "Dick seems to be Bobby's fiery steed at the moment."

In another minute Bobby burst into the kitchen followed by his older brother. "Dick and me," the little boy yelled excitedly, "has another see-crud."

"Dick and I have," his mother corrected him patiently. "Come here, Bobby, and let me wash your hands. You're really naughty, you know. You should have come home when Brian and Mart did."

"Couldn't," Bobby said loftily. "They wented home too soon. I was busy."

"Oh, yeah?" Mart gently pulled one of Bobby's yellow curls. "Busy as a bear in the wintertime, I suppose."

"Was so busy," Bobby said, raising his voice. "I was helping Dick. We had to clean the cars. He's going away this afternoon."

"Where to?" Trixie asked suspiciously. "He isn't

due for a day off yet. He just started to work yesterday."

"He's got the day off," Bobby informed her as he climbed into his chair at the table. "He axed Miss Trask, and she said he could. But he's gotta come back tonight."

"How do you like that?" Mart asked Brian. "If Dick gets half a day off every other day, he'll soon be owing Mr. Wheeler money. Chauffeurs, I gather from Jim, get paid in advance, unlike junior counselors."

Mrs. Belden laughed and handed him a plate heaped high with macaroni and cheese. "From the way you talk, Mart, one would think you'd been worked to death this summer," she said. "I happen to know better."

Mart chuckled. "Can't a man get any sympathy from his own mother?"

"Not in this case," Mrs. Belden said firmly.

"If anyone deserves sympathy," Trixie put in, "it's me; I mean, I. Work, work, work, that's all I've done the whole livelong summer."

Brian howled with laughter. "How about that trailer trip, honey chile? And when did you find time to learn to ride and improve your crawl stroke?"

They all laughed, then, and after lunch the boys insisted upon washing and drying the dishes. "We're more efficient than you," Mart told Trixie, "so we'll get through sooner." He added in a whisper, "Scram. Honey is dying to tell you the latest dope."

Trixie needed no further urging. She dashed out of the kitchen, hopped over the terrace wall, and tore across the fields to the path. At the top of the hill, she met Honey on her way down.

"Did you get a chance to talk with Brian and Mart?" Honey asked immediately.

Trixie shook her head. "Moms was around all the time. What's the news? Did you show them our clues?"

"I tried to," Honey said, "but there weren't any left. Someone had walked all over the heelmarks in the cottage, and another car had driven over the clues down by the road."

"How about the footprints in the thicket?" Trixie asked wonderingly.

"They were crisscrossed with other footprints," Honey said forlornly. "And all of them were so messy you couldn't really tell a thing, even though we examined them carefully with flashlights." She sighed. "I suppose Nailor messed up the clues on the cottage floor. He was mowing down near the cottage this morning, and, after all, we left the door wide open; so I imagine he got curious and went inside."

"I guess so," Trixie said in a depressed tone of

voice. "And somebody driving north along the road must have pulled off to the side to change a tire or something. Just our luck that he had to park on top of our clues."

"Well, anyway," Honey said, trying to be cheerful, "Miss Trask wasn't at all suspicious when Jim and I asked her if we could change rooms. She said changes of one's environment were always very good for one."

"I've heard the word mentioned," Trixie said, "but I don't know what it means, exactly. Your surroundings?"

"That's right," Honey said. "What did you think of Dick's black eye?"

"On him," Trixie said with a sniff, "it looked swell. And I liked his battered mouth, too. Did he try to tell you that Jupe kicked him?"

"He didn't say anything to me about it at all," Honey said. "And I don't know what excuse he gave Miss Trask. Anyway, she gave him the afternoon off, so he could go see his doctor in New York. He just drove off in his own car."

"What time is he coming back?" Trixie asked. "In time to walk into our trap, I hope."

"He said he'd be back late this afternoon or early this evening," Honey said. "But, of course, that depends on what his doctor says. If his eye closes completely, he really shouldn't drive a car. I hope he isn't laid up for long. He's going to give Jim driving lessons right away, you know."

"I didn't know," Trixie said. "Did he suggest the idea himself, or did Miss Trask order him to do it?"

"Oh, it was Dick's idea," Honey said. "He's really very nice and polite to me and Jim. Just before he left, he asked Jim if he knew how to drive; and when Jim said he didn't, he offered to teach him."

"Well, well, well," Trixie said. "I guess I'm the only one on his hate list. And I couldn't care less." She disconsolately kicked a pebble on the driveway. "I wish we dared go search his room for clues."

"Oh, we couldn't possibly do that," Honey cried.

"I know, I know," Trixie moaned; "but I can dream, can't I?" Suddenly, she grabbed Honey's arm. "We can search the grounds for clues, can't we? I mean, suppose we found footprints with rubber heels to match the other ones?"

"What a wonderful idea," Honey said. "Where'll we start?"

"Wherever Dick may have been walking," Trixie replied promptly.

Honey sighed. "As far as I know, he's only walked across the driveway from the garage to the kitchen door when he went inside for meals. We can't hope to find footprints in the gravel."

"Don't be silly," Trixie said. "Bobby showed him all over the place yesterday. They couldn't have kept to the driveway or the lawns all the time. Not with Bobby conducting the sightseeing tour. Let's look in all the flower beds."

Honey laughed. "Even if we should find footprints in the flower beds, it won't prove anything. They could have been made by Gallagher."

"True, too true," Trixie said with a groan. "I give up."

Jim came down the front steps, then. "Why so gloomy, girls?"

"Why so cheery?" Trixie came back at him. "All our clues ruined!"

"They didn't amount to a row of pins, anyway," Jim said. "Not to us, anyway. Police detectives could probably have learned a lot from the tire treadmarks and rubber-heeled imprints, but we haven't a crime lab." He grinned at Trixie. "A lot of people have rubber heels on their shoes and drive cars with rubber tires."

Suddenly, Trixie remembered something. "Honey," she hissed. "Where is the diamond, now?"

Honey turned pale. "I d-don't know. The l-last time I had it was down by your chicken coop. Everyone was

taking turns looking at it while you were telling your brothers how we found it." She clutched Jim's arm. "Oh, OH! Suppose somebody dropped it in that long grass."

Trixie felt sick and weak with worry. "A crow has probably made off with it by now, Honey; and I know about crows. They can't resist anything that glitters."

"Hold your horses," Jim said. "Even a crow's sharp eyes couldn't see through that long grass. Let's get down and have a look before we jump to conclusions."

"I can't take a step," Trixie said, collapsing on the lawn. "My knees are shaking, and I've got butterflies in my stomach. I just know we'll never see that diamond again."

Honey sank down beside her. "I can't move, either. Oh, why didn't I leave it in my jewelry box?"

Jim stared at them with disgust. "Pull yourselves together," he said sternly. "There's no point in crossing bridges until you come to them. A fine pair of female detectives you two are going to make!"

Trixie immediately scrambled to her feet, her cheeks flaming. "You're absolutely right, Jim," she said coldly. "The diamond is probably perfectly safe. Come on, Honey, let's go find it. It's our worry, not Jim's."

"Temper, temper," Jim said, helping Honey to her feet. "We'll all go look. We're all in this mess, now. If it's lost, it's as much my fault as yours. I should have made you turn it over to the police."

"I hope it is lost," Honey said suddenly. "I never want to see the horrid thing again. It's practically ruined my whole summer."

Jim hooted. "This is Friday afternoon, and you found it Wednesday morning. What brief summers you have, Miss Wheeler!"

Honey giggled nervously. "Oh, you know what I mean, Jim. Anyway, if it is lost, who's going to know that we lost it?"

"Or found it, for that matter," Trixie said, cheering up. "I'm sure Dick stole it, so it certainly doesn't belong to him."

"It belongs to somebody," Jim pointed out as they hurried down the path to the hollow. "And that some-body must have notified the police when it was stolen. We can be pretty sure of that."

"Then you agree with us now?" Trixie asked tri-umphantly. "It was stolen, and whoever stole it dropped it in the cottage?"

"I don't know what else to believe," Jim admitted. "But any way you look at it, whether it was lost or stolen, whoever owns it must have notified the police right away. Sooner or later, detectives are going to show up in this neck of the woods and start asking questions. In fact, I'm surprised that they haven't yet."

"Maybe Dick's a plain-clothes man in disguise," Honey interrupted. "Maybe he got that black eye fighting with the man who tried to sneak into my room last night. Maybe he captured him and took him to the police station last night. Maybe the man has confessed that he stole the diamond; but he lost it and we found it. Oh, oh," she finished, "now what'll we do?"

Trixie stuck her fingers in her ears. "Don't talk like that, Honey," she begged. "I can't stand it."

"Whoa, both of you," Jim said. "Curb your imaginations. We don't even know for sure that it was a man who tried to sneak into your room last night, Honey. It might have been one of the maids. Helen, for instance. Miss Trask just hired her on Monday. Suppose she took a walk through the woods Wednesday and saw you go into the cottage? It might have been she who listened in the thicket and heard you say that you had put it in your jewelry box. She could have come back last night and sneaked into the house. It's only a two-mile walk from the village."

Honey stared at him. "You don't really suspect Helen, do you, Jim? She could have stolen the diamond in the daytime when she cleaned the bedrooms."

Jim grinned. "I don't really suspect anybody. I'm just trying to show you two girl-detectives that a lot of people besides Dick and Nailor may know that you found the diamond in the cottage. Gallagher, for instance. Don't you think it's suspicious that he quit the very day you found it? Why should he get mad just because you walked off with his pruning saws and shovels? There's no pruning to be done at this time of the year."

"He was doing a lot of transplanting," Honey said. "Maybe he needed the shovels."

"Normal people," Jim told her, "use spades when they dig holes in the ground. They use shovels when they want to clear away coal or dirt and things like that. Next time you decide to look for buried treasure, take spades."

"Thanks for the information," Trixie said. "And stop trying to make us suspect Gallagher. If he snooped around the cottage Wednesday and heard that we'd found a valuable diamond, the last thing he would have done was quit. He would have stayed on hoping for a chance to get into the house, so he could swipe it." She got down on her hands and knees and began to peer into the long grass by the chicken coop. "Let's crawl while we look for it, instead of walking," she said. "If we walk on it, we might trample it so deeply into the ground that it never can be found."

"That's right," Honey agreed. "If we crawl on it, we'll feel it with our knees like Bobby did."

They searched in silence for a while and then Jim said, "A perfectly ordinary tramp, who had nothing to do with the theft of the diamond, might have been strolling along Glen Road Wednesday morning. When he passed the cottage, he might have heard you talking and decided to eavesdrop just out of curiosity."

"Oh, stop it, Jim," Trixie begged. "No ordinary tramp tried to sneak into Honey's room last night. How could he have possibly known which room was hers?"

"You've got me there," Jim admitted, "but here's another idea. Maybe Brian tucked the diamond in the pocket of his swimming trunks—or Mart."

"Don't even say such a thing," Honey wailed. "If we have to comb the bottom of the lake, I'll drown myself right now."

"You're a good enough diver to find it," Jim said, "but what I'm trying to say is that the diamond may still be in the pocket."

"We wouldn't have any such luck," Trixie moaned. "Even if Brian put it in his pocket and buttoned the flap, a snapping turtle got it out, somehow."

Honey giggled. "Go on into the house and ask your brothers, Trixie. One of them may know where it is."

"Here they come now," Trixie said. "All three of them. Be careful what you say in front of Bobby unless you want the whole Sleepyside police force out here asking us embarrassing questions."

"What cooks, gang?" Mart asked when he came closer to the rock where Trixie had perched that morning. "Haven't you got anything more exciting to do than look for four-leaf clovers?"

Trixie coughed loudly. "That's just what we're looking for. A clover with facets. Facets. Have you got it, Mart?"

Mart stared at her, and Bobby promptly said, "I know what a facet is. I washed my hands under the kitchen facet when I got through making mud pies."

"Fine," Trixie said. "Now go back and wash them again. Your fingernails are dirty."

"Are not!" Bobby yelled. "Yours are."

"So they are," Trixie admitted. "Run in the house and get me a nail file, will you, please, Bobby darling?"

"No," Bobby said firmly. "Go get it your own self."

Trixie turned to Brian with a hopeless expression on her face. "Have you by any chance got you-know-what?"

For answer, Brian turned the pockets of his jeans inside out, and Mart followed suit.

"This is the end," Trixie gasped, sinking down on the rock.

"It would help," Mart said, "if we knew what you were looking for."

Then Jim got an idea. "A famous, very rich man, with the same first name as mine, collected jewels and got himself a nickname. Guess who?"

"James Buchanan Brady," Brian said promptly, "more commonly known as Di—"

Trixie was seized with a violent fit of coughing then; Honey hummed loudly, and Jim whistled shrilly through his fingers.

"Gleeps," Mart yelled. "I get it. Oh, *no!*"

"Oh, *yes,*" Trixie said. "And we've combed every inch of the grass around this rock. Now what?"

Chapter 9
A Search

It was Bobby who broke the silence. "Hey!" he shouted. "I founded a four-leaf clover."

Trixie glared at him. "Don't be so silly. You can count. It's only got three leaves."

"Has not," Bobby corrected. "I never touch anything with three leaves. Might be poison ivy."

"Good for you," Mart said, lifting the little boy into his arms. "If the kids I took care of at camp had your brains, I wouldn't have spent so much time drowning them in calamine lotion."

"He is smart," Trixie admitted, and added shrewdly, "Bobby, why don't you show Mart the outdoor shower Jim rigged up for you?"

"You're wasting your breath," Mart said as Bobby wriggled out of his arms. "I know that age. They stick like burs when you want to get away from them, and disappear like magic at bedtime."

"There must be some way we can have a conference," Brian said thoughtfully. "Don't you take a nap any more, Bobby?"

"He does," Trixie said wearily, "but this being your first day home, Moms let him off. If only we could all speak French, like Honey. For the first time in my life, I wish our parents had been rich enough to send us to boarding school."

"I know what," Honey said suddenly. "Miss Trask! She's teaching Bobby how to add and subtract with little stones. Wouldn't you like to play with Miss Trask for a while, Bobby?"

"Yeah," Bobby cried enthusiastically. "I founded a pretty, great big stone right here this morning. Wait! I'll go get it for Miss Trask."

He started off but Trixie grabbed his arm. "You found *what* here?"

"Hey!" he yelled. "Lemme go. You hurted my arm, *bad*ly." He pulled away from her and raced across the field toward the house.

"See what I mean?" Mart asked with a shrug. "As soon as you want them for anything, you find that they're allergic to you. It never fails."

"This is no time for joking," Trixie said briskly. "Don't you realize that Bobby found the diamond?"

"Gleeps," Mart howled. "The pretty, great big stone! Let's go after him, Trix."

"Take it easy, kids," Brian interrupted. "You'll only

stampede him if you rush after him. Let him bring it back."

"That's right," Jim agreed. "If you start asking him a lot of questions, he might get so confused he'll forget where he put it."

"The suspense is maddening," Trixie moaned, collapsing on the rock again. "It would be just like Bobby to have dropped it down the drain when he washed his hands at the kitchen *facet.*"

"I'm not even going to think until he comes back," Honey said. "Suppose he shows up with a plain ordinary rock? Suppose he made it into a mud pie and threw it into the pond? That pond is knee-deep in mud."

"I thought you weren't going to think," Jim reminded her with a grin. "If you must do it, don't do it out loud. It gives me the jitters to think of what he might have done with the diamond."

"The only bright spot," Trixie said, "is that he didn't give it to Dick, his bosom friend."

"Oh-h-h," Mart sighed loudly. "Maybe he did. Maybe that's why Dick scrammed."

Trixie covered her face with her hands, rocking back and forth. "Now we *will* go to jail, not only for withholding information, but for aiding and abetting a criminal. If only I'd let Honey give the thing to her father the minute we found it."

"There's no sense in crying over spilled milk," Brian said sharply. "Here comes Bobby, and he *is* crying, so I guess he doesn't know where he put it."

"I losted it, I losted it," Bobby was screaming at the top of his lungs. "Holp! Holp!"

"Help, help, yourself," Trixie muttered under her breath. "Oh, why do I get myself into these scrapes?"

"That's not the question I'm asking myself," Brian said bitterly. "What I want to know is how you always manage to get us in Dutch with you?"

"Oh, go away," Trixie said, on the verge of tears. "Go back to camp. Go join the Navy. I don't care what happens now."

"Oh, Trixie," Honey cried, joining her on the rock. "Don't feel so badly. Daddy has plenty of money. He can keep us out of jail." She threw her slender arms around Trixie. "If the police come around asking for diamonds, Mother will give them one of hers."

"Thanks, Honey," Trixie said forlornly, "but that's out." She got up, squaring her shoulders and said to Bobby, "Stop bawling. Tell us where you put the pretty stone, and we'll all help you find it."

Bobby kept right on screaming, and she added in a more gentle voice, "It'll be our secret. A *secret,* Bobby. Nobody will know about it but you and me and Brian

118

and Mart and Honey and Jim. A *real* secret."

Instantly the little boy was all smiles. "A real see-crud, Trixie?"

"That's right," Mart said. "Wild horses couldn't drag it out of me. Where did you take the pretty stone after you found it, Bobby?"

"To the sandpile," he said promptly. "The one Jim made for me by the shower."

"That'll teach you," Mart said in an aside to Jim. "Never be kind to this age group." He grinned, cuddling Bobby closer to him. "And after the sandpile, Little King? Mud pies?"

"Oh, no," Bobby said airily. "I put in my pocket." He turned one pocket of his playsuit inside out, displaying a large hole. "But it wented out."

"Where?" Trixie asked dismally. "While you were catching frogs in the pond?"

He nodded his head up and down, and Trixie held her breath. "But I found it again with my strainer," he told her. "And *then,* I put it in this pocket, so it wouldn't get losted. And *then,* I went up to see Dickie. Mummy said I could," he added defensively. "You were down in the garden."

"Never mind where Trixie was," Brian said, smiling down at his little brother. "We're only interested in where *you* were all day. Did you show Dick the pretty stone?"

"No," Bobby admitted sadly. "I forgot."

"Did you put it somewhere in my room," Honey asked, "while you helped Jim and me move our things?"

"I don't *think* so," Bobby said, frowning. "I put it in Jim's camera, oncet, but I tooked it out again."

"Inside my tennis racket case, maybe?" Jim asked. "In the pocket where I keep the balls I said you could have?"

"I don't *think* so," Bobby said again. "I think I put it in a box. A sort of boxlike thing. But maybe I put it in my teddy bear. He's got a big hole in his head."

"We've all got holes in our heads," Mart said sorrowfully. "Which one of us masterminds dropped it here in the grass?"

"*I* dropped it lots of times," Bobby informed him cheerfully. "But it's so shiny, I always founded it again."

"I tell you what," Mart said. "I'll give you a shiny, bright, glittery-like dime if you find it. Why don't you go get your teddy bear and see it it's in his head?"

"Okey, dokey," Bobby said and scampered off.

The minute he was out of earshot, they all spoke at once.

"It's somewhere in my room," Honey said.

"I'll bet it's in with my fishing tackle," Jim said.

"It's in the bottom of the pond," Trixie said.

"I'm going to sift the sandpile with a strainer," Brian said.

"The place to look," Mart said, "is in the mud under his shower."

"What did you say?" they all asked each other.

Brian held up his hand. "Let's not do that all over again. This Tower of Babel business will get us nowhere. Let's all go and look wherever we think it might be. And report at the boathouse in an hour."

"It might be in his teddy bear," Honey said.

"Not a prayer," Trixie told her. "If we'd found a four-leaf clover, yes. But with only crabgrass on our side, no." She started off for the little pond below the rock garden. "If I don't show up in an hour, you'll know I met the same fate as 'Clementine.' "

"We'll see that you get a decent burial," Mart called after her.

"Don't bother," Trixie retorted. "If I don't find that diamond, I'll dig my own grave."

An hour later, they all met at the rustic boathouse by the lake. "Don't let's say anything," Trixie said. "I can tell from the expression on your faces that you didn't find it."

"You look so cheery," Mart said, "I'm sure *you* found it."

"I did," Trixie said. "But when I'd dug my way clear through to China, I found that a little boy there had found it in a rice field. He needed it more than I did, so I let him keep it."

"That was real generous of you," Jim said. "I hope he brings you rice cakes in jail."

"I don't know how you can joke about it," Honey said. "I searched every inch of my room. I mean Jim's room. Oh, what do I mean?"

"It doesn't matter," Trixie said sourly. "If I had a grappling iron, I'd search the bottom of the lake, just for the fun of it."

"I, at least," Mart put in, "had sense enough to check up on the teddy bear angle. No soap."

"If you had any sense," Trixie said, "you'd check up on the Dick angle. That guy probably picked Bobby's pocket."

"Oh, come, come," Jim said. "Let's not go off on tangents. Dick isn't really a bad guy, Trixie. Just because you don't get on with him doesn't mean he's a dip."

"A what?" Trixie demanded. "Did you say a dip? Drip is the word."

"Dip," Mart explained. "It's short for pickpocket. Don't ask me why. It's gangster lingo."

Trixie arched her eyebrows at him. "What nice bits

of language you picked up at camp. Did one of the small fry teach you?"

"No," Mart said grinning. "State troopers. They stopped us just when we were starting down the river. Wanted to know if we'd noticed any strangers lurking around the woods near camp. They're on the trail of two famous dips."

"That word grows on you," Trixie said. "Pretty soon, you'll be talking out of the corner of your mouth. Dip," she repeated. "It sounds better when you say, Dick the Dip. Maybe he's one of your pickpockets."

"Oh, undoubtedly," Mart said. "To be sure, to be sure. And he specializes in picking the pockets of fat little boys in playsuits."

"Dick the Dick sounds better to me," Honey said with a giggle. "I'm sure he's a detective."

"A G-man, no less," Trixie jeered. "It's well known that they all look like weasels."

"Let's make some sense for a change," Jim interrupted. "Where else should we look? I'm serious. We've got to find it. It doesn't belong to us, and it does belong to someone."

"Don't rub it in," Trixie moaned. "Where do *you* think we should look? And don't say anything about mud pies. I examined that angle thoroughly, as well as Bobby's room and his toy box."

"All that and China, too?" Mart demanded. "My, what a fast worker you are, grandma."

"The pond isn't very big," Trixie reminded him. "And neither is Bobby's room. The toy box was the worst part of it." Suddenly she jumped up. "Box, that's it. Remember? He said he put it in a sort of boxlike thing." She turned to Honey. "Did you look in your jewelry box?"

"Of course not," Honey said. "It's in Jim's room. I mean, my old room."

"I didn't look in it, either," Jim admitted. "Do you really think that's where it is, Trixie?"

"I'm almost sure of it," Trixie cried. "Bobby adores boxes. He simply can't resist them. He's forever filling the ones in our house with rubber bands and paper clips and stubs of pencils. Shiny stones, too. Come *on!*"

She raced up the path and they all hurried after her. Upstairs in Honey's former room, they saw that the jewelry box was still on the dressing table where she and Jim had carefully left it.

Honey lifted the lid. "Nothing but costume jewelry." She took out the tray. "It's not here."

"Try the secret compartment," Trixie said. "When his fat little hands go exploring, they don't miss a thing."

Honey slipped her hand under the box and one small section of the bottom sprang open. She gasped. "It's there—in the secret compartment. How on earth did he find it?"

Trixie grabbed the diamond and clutched it tightly in one hand. "Bobby," she said weakly, "can find anything if you don't want him to find it."

"How do you like that?" Mart demanded. "Traveling along devious routes, he brought it right back to the exact place from which Honey had just taken it!"

"And for that," Trixie said, "I'll never say another cross word to him."

Chapter 10
A House Party

"Well, now that we've found it for the second time," Honey said, "where are we going to keep it?"

"Down at our house," Mart said promptly. "That's almost the best part of not being rich. Burglars never bother us."

"Okay," Jim agreed. "Whereabouts in your house? We don't want Bobby to find it again."

"Heaven forbid," Brian groaned. "How about in the toe of my old riding boots that are too small for me and still too big for Mart?"

"That's as safe a place as any," Trixie said. "*If* you put them on the top shelf of your closet, way, way back."

"Of course," Jim said slowly, "the sensible thing to do is to turn it over to the police right now."

"Let's not be sensible for a while," Trixie said. "Suppose one of the men who stole the diamond walks into our trap tonight, and you catch him red-handed, Jim. Then the police will love us. But, if we give them the diamond before we've solved the mystery, we won't be so popular, especially now that all the clues have been ruined."

"Obliterated is the word," Brian said. "And annihilated is a good word to describe the condition we'll be in after we get through trying to explain to the authorities why we kept the diamond so long."

Honey tossed her long hair. "I don't care. After all the agony I've been through worrying over that horrid thing, I don't think we should give it to anybody until we've at least tried to find out who stole it."

Mart chuckled. "I'm for forgetting all rules and regulations except the one that says finders are keepers for a few days more, anyway."

"You've got a point there," Brian said. "The person who left the diamond in the cottage, accidentally or on purpose, was trespassing. Isn't there some law which says finders *are* keepers if you find something on your own property, Jim?"

"I think so," Jim said thoughtfully. "Suppose we struck oil. It would belong to us, not to the descendants of the family that originally purchased this land from the State of New York after the Revolution."

"Now I feel better," Honey said. "Although I wouldn't have the thing as a gift. Besides, we're really trying to help the police, and we actually have helped them, in a way. That is, if Trixie's theory is correct."

"Let's hear Trixie's theory again," Mart said. "But let's get cooled off. Can you lend Brian and me trunks, Jim?"

"Sure," Jim said. "Let's see, where are my swimming trunks, Honey?"

"I don't know where anything is any more," Honey complained. "I moved some of my things to your old room, but not all of them."

"Me, too," Jim said, grinning. He pulled a long mirror away from the wall, revealing several rows of shelves. "Yours, all yours, Honey. I guess my extra trunks are in the other room."

"Well, hurry up and change," Honey said. "I'll lend Trixie a bathing suit, and we'll meet you down at the boathouse in five minutes."

"Wait a minute," Trixie said, holding her hands behind her back. "Diamond, diamond, who's got the diamond?"

"You have," Brian said, smiling. "Run home and put it in the toe of my riding boot like a good girl."

"I'll do nothing of the kind," Trixie retorted. "If I so much as darken our door, Moms will think up seventy million chores for me to do. I slaved all morning. *You* go."

"I tell you what," Mart said cheerfully. "I'll try to

guess which of your dirty little paws is clutching the joo-well. If I guess wrong, I'll take it home."

"Okay," Trixie agreed. "Right or left?"

"Right," Mart said.

"Wrong," Trixie said and gave him the diamond. "Run along, Mart dear, and don't forget to feed the chickens and gather the eggs."

"Oh, brother," Mart groaned. "I forgot that item."

"They need fresh water, too," Trixie said gaily. "Lucky for you, Jim filled the mash hoppers this morning. If I were you, I'd hurry like anything. Dad will be home any minute, and if he sees you, he may suggest that the coop needs cleaning out and fresh litter put in."

Mart raced off with a faint moan, and Trixie turned to Jim. "For your information, smarty, shovels are also used for cleaning out chicken coops, not spades."

Jim chortled. "My, how you hate to be made fun of, Miss Belden. For your own information, I know more about the care and feeding of poultry than you ever will know."

"Keep it to yourself," Trixie said tartly. "What I've been through this summer has turned me against chickens and eggs in any form."

"Oh, dear," Honey wailed. "Miss Trask wants all of

you to have dinner with us tonight and spend the night, too. Sort of a welcome-home house party for your brothers, Trixie, but we're going to have fried chicken."

"That's different," Trixie said quickly. "As long as they're not our chickens."

Jim gave Honey a surprised look. "How clever you are, little stepsister. When did you arrange to have all hands on deck for the springing of the trap tonight?"

Honey patted herself on the shoulder. "I *am* smart. I thought it was a good idea to have, as you say, all hands on deck. That prowler can't possibly get away from all of us." She giggled. "To be honest, it was Miss Trask's idea, not mine—the house party. It's to last the whole weekend."

Trixie collapsed on Honey's big bed. "I can't stand it. It's too good to be true. Did Moms agree?"

"She certainly did," Honey informed her with a gay smile. "She said you deserved a vacation. And guess what?"

"One thing at a time, puh-leeze," Brian begged. "Does Miss Trask really want all three of us Beldens eating you out of house and home for forty-eight hours? And have you enough room?"

"Of course," Honey said. "Miss Trask is very thrilled about the whole thing. There are twin beds in

Jim's old room for Trixie and me. It's across the hall. And right next to it is another room with twin beds for you and Mart."

Trixie hugged her impulsively. "Oh, Honey, it's the nicest thing that ever happened to us."

"It was supposed to be a surprise," Honey said, "until the last minute. But when Mart looked so depressed about cleaning the chicken coop, I couldn't stand it. He'll be back soon, I'm sure, with a suitcase which your mother already packed with whatever clothes you'll need."

"Moms," Trixie cried, "is an angel. She's much too good to me. I don't deserve it. I'm always complaining."

Brian patted her arm affectionately. "You're not so bad, Sis. Dad is very proud of you. He was telling us how hard you've worked to earn the money for Jed Tomlin's colt."

"I wish I had my own horse right now," Trixie said. "Then we could all go riding this evening when it gets cooler."

"That's the best surprise of all," Honey said smugly. "There are five horses in the stable right now. Miss Trask arranged with Mr. Tomlin to rent us that sweet little black mare for the weekend. You remember Susie, Trixie?"

"Oh, oh," Trixie cried. "I fell in love with her the day we went over there with your father and Jim to look at horses. Is Susie really in the stable now?"

"I think so," Honey said. "Anyway, if she isn't, Regan will go and get her. He's due back from his day off on the six o'clock train. He can ride over to Mr. Tomlin's on Jupe and lead Susie back."

"I can do it for that matter," Brian offered. "It's only a three-mile round trip. Gosh," he finished, "I'm dying to meet Regan."

"He's a great guy," Jim said. "And let's give him a break. Let's go down to the stable and see if Susie has arrived. If she hasn't, you and I can go get her. I'll ride Jupe, and you can take the new horse, Starlight. He's a chestnut gelding, and I think you'll like him, Brian."

"Great," Brian said. "Let's go. We don't need to bother with boots, do we? I outgrew mine this summer."

"Boots," Jim said with a grin. "What are they? Only Dad and Mother wear 'em around here."

After the boys left, Trixie and Honey changed into swim suits. When they came down to the porch, they saw Jim and Brian riding down the driveway. Then Mart came into sight carrying a suitcase.

"Gleeps, creeps, and weeps," he shouted. "Have you heard about the house party, Trix?"

"Isn't it super?" she asked. "Did you run into Dad, and what did he say?"

"He arrived just as I was leaving, and he thought the whole idea was great." Mart hurried inside with the suitcase and came back in a few minutes wearing his swimming trunks. "Where are Jim and Brian?"

The girls explained on the way to the boathouse.

"This is too much," Mart exploded. "Gosh, Honey, can we all go for a ride through the woods this evening?"

Honey nodded and slipped a cap on over her shiny, brown hair. "We're going to have dinner early especially so we can ride around eight when it begins to cool off. And we can take one last dip in the lake after that if we want to. And tomorrow morning we can ride or swim before breakfast, or both. Miss Trask thought we might like to fix our own breakfast down here on the grill. There's a waffle-iron somewhere around and skewers so we can barbecue tomatoes wrapped in bacon slices."

"Yummy-yum-*yum.*" Trixie licked her lips and blinked her blue eyes. Mart pushed her off the diving board. Then Honey pushed him off, lost her balance, and fell in. But she beat them all to the raft.

There, they stretched out in the late afternoon sun, and Mart said, "Let's hear your theory of how the diamond and the footprints came into our lives, Trix. I want

134

to know why Honey thinks the police are going to love us when we confess."

"Well," Trixie began, "suppose two robbers spent Tuesday night in the cottage. Then they had a fight. The dirt floor was plenty scuffed. During the battle, one of them dropped the diamond and it got ground into the mud. They left; and when they realized it was missing from their loot, they came back. But," she summed it up, "we had already found it. So you see, if it hadn't been for us, the thieves would have it. That's what Honey means when she said we have already helped the police."

"From you," Mart said, "it sounds swell. But a police dick could find a million holes in that theory."

"How slangy can we get?" Trixie demanded. "All we seem to talk about these days are dicks and dips. Jim had the nerve to say that when Honey and I open our detective agency, we'd call ourselves Moll Dicks, Incorporated."

Honey giggled. "It grows on you. I'm beginning to like it. Moll Dicks. Um-m-m. What do you think, Mart?"

"I think," Mart said, "that you girls had better stick to your knitting. Not that Trixie knows the difference between a p-u-r-l and a p-e-a-r-l."

"And I hope I never learn," Trixie said with a sniff.

135

"I hate needles and jewelry, especially diamonds, at the moment. By the way, is it where it should be, or did you feed it to the chickens by mistake?"

"I wish I'd thought of that," Mart said dreamily. "A chicken's crop would be the safest place in the world. No, it's not where it should be."

"Why not?" Trixie demanded.

"Because," Mart said, "Moms had already packed Brian's boots in the bottom of the suitcase. She didn't know they're too small for him, and I didn't have the heart to tell her."

"Don't keep us in suspense," Trixie shouted. "WHERE IS IT?"

Mart rubbed his chin with his thumb. "I think I'll have to start shaving soon," he said thoughtfully. "Have I got a five o'clock shadow, Honey?"

Honey shook with laughter. "No, old man," she told him, "you've got a long gray beard, and it's very becoming."

"Stop it," Trixie interrupted. "I wish you did have some hair on your chin, Mart Belden. I'd yank it out by the roots."

He rolled off the raft and came up gurgling. "Help. Or, as Bobby would say, holp!"

Trixie and Honey dove off and ducked him.

"Please, Mart, puh-leeze," Trixie begged. "Tell us where you put the diamond."

"We'll drown you, if you don't," Honey warned.

Mart promptly climbed up the ladder and they followed. "It couldn't be in a safer place," he said. "Remember that sewing basket some poor deluded female relative gave you last Christmas, Trixie?"

Trixie nodded. "Aunt Alicia. She tried to teach me how to tat when I was eight. You would think she would have learned after that horrible experience. What about my so-called sewing basket? I don't even know where it is."

"I do," Mart said. "It's in the attic. When I lifted the top, after brushing away several yards of cobwebs, a few moths flew out. So I said to myself, 'If only moths frequent this spot, this is it.' Upon further examination, I deducted that, at one time, the strawberry-shaped pin-cushion must have come in contact with Bobby, for it, too, had a hole in its head. So I thrust the diamond inside it, replaced the top on the basket—and the cobwebs—and dashed downstairs without arousing anyone's suspicions."

Trixie sneered. "Says you! Where, pray tell, was Bobby while you were exploring the jungles of the attic with rod and camera?"

Mart gave her a superior glance. "In his room replacing the toys you flung out of his toy box. Brother, is he furious! Revenge, he tells me, will be sweet. Saccharine-sweet!"

Trixie bit her lip. "I meant to put all that junk back, but it hardly seemed worthwhile. Even the blocks looked as though rats had been gnawing them. Is Moms mad at me?"

Mart shrugged. "We had hardly time to discuss your tidy nature, our mother and I, but Bobby is not mad. He is wild. Especially since he was assigned the chore of making his small room navigable again."

Trixie tossed her damp, blond curls. "Serves him right. He's wrecked my room plenty of times, and I had to pick up the pieces."

"Well, anyway," Honey put in, "it's good to know that the diamond is in a safe place."

"I'm not at all sure of that," Trixie said worriedly. "Suppose Bobby decides to throw my sewing basket into the trash can for spite? He's too young to know that I despise the thing."

"Pooh, pooh," Mart said airily. "He probably has no idea that it belongs to you. From the evidence, I would say that it was relegated to the attic on Christmas night."

"Stop using big words," Trixie said crossly. "It's getting on my nerves. I wish I knew exactly when I did put that sewing basket up in the attic. Moths didn't really fly out when you opened it, did they, Mart?"

"That," he admitted, "was a slight exaggeration. But the cobwebs were not exaggerated."

"They mean nothing," Trixie said. "They grow like weeds during the hot summer weather."

"They don't grow," Mart corrected her. "If you had my superior education, you would know that they are spun."

Trixie ignored him. "I think I'd better go home," she said, "and put that diamond in another place. I don't trust Bobby. I don't trust him when he's in a sunny mood, and if he's sulking, well, anything could happen."

She dove off the raft and swam back to the boathouse.

Chapter 11
Regan Has a Secret

But Trixie did not go straight home, after all. By the time she had changed into dungarees and a clean shirt, Brian and Jim had come back with the rented horse.

Trixie met them as she was crossing the driveway on her way to the path that led down to the hollow. The sight of the lovely little black mare drove all other thoughts from her mind.

"Oh, Susie," she cried, throwing her arms around the horse's glossy neck. "You lovely, beautiful, gorgeous thing! Please, Jim, may I ride her right this minute?"

"No bareback riding on rented horses," a voice said from the stable. Regan joined them, grinning.

"Oh, Regan," Trixie said. "I'm so glad you're back. This is my brother, Brian."

Brian leaned down from the saddle to shake hands with the pleasant-faced groom. "Boy, it's great to meet you, Regan."

"The pleasure is mine," Regan said with a friendly smile. "Is Mart the blond boy with the crew cut who's down at the boathouse with Honey?"

"That's right," Trixie said.

"Except for a difference in height," Regan said, "you look enough alike to be twins. But you and Brian don't look at all alike. You take after your father, don't you, fella?" he asked Brian.

Brian nodded. "I'm supposed to."

"It's hard to believe," Trixie teased. "Dad's a very good-looking man."

"And your mother is a very pretty lady," Regan said. "It kills me to admit it, Trixie, but you look enough like her to be her own daughter." His green eyes twinkled. "If you ever become a lady, which I very much doubt, people might even call you pretty."

"I have no intention of becoming a lady," Trixie said impudently. "Ladies sit around sewing—" She stopped, remembering where the diamond was.

"You couldn't sit still long enough to thread a needle," Regan was saying in his cheerful voice. "Some day you're going to have to acquire patience. All you kids should learn to drive cars while you're in high school. Hear Dick's going to give you a lesson tomorrow, right?" he asked Jim.

"That's right," Jim said. "If he gets back."

"And why shouldn't he be back tonight?" Regan demanded, his freckled hands on his hips. "What's a black eye? I've had many a shiner in my time and never took up a busy doctor's time with it."

Mart and Honey joined the little group in front of the stable then. After Mart had been introduced to Regan, he said, "Do I smell fried chicken, or is it wishful thinking?"

Honey sniffed. A delicious odor was wafting out from the kitchen. "You smell correctly," she told Mart. "Dinner must be almost ready. Come on, we'd better change into dry clothes."

Regan's sandy eyebrows shot up with surprise. "Dinner at this unfashionable hour, Honey?" he asked. "Since when? It's only six-thirty."

"Just for tonight," Honey explained. "We want to go for a ride through the woods at eight, if it's all right with you, Regan."

"It's fine with me," he said, "if you all groom your horses when you come back. I've got to drive Celia and the cook into the village, if Dick doesn't show up, and drive them back again. They're going to the movie at the Cameo. Thought you kids might be planning to take it in, too."

"We're going tomorrow night," Honey told him. "The radio said it's going to rain, so we thought we'd better ride while we can."

"The horses need exercise, all right," Regan said. "What's the matter with you kids? You used to live in the saddle."

"It's been so hot," Honey explained quickly. "But now that Brian and Mart are home, we'll be sure to ride the horses enough. We'll take turns after Susie goes back to Mr. Tomlin."

"I have a feeling Susie is here to stay," Regan said mysteriously.

"Oh, Regan," Trixie cried excitedly. "What makes you think so?"

He hummed softly to himself and strode into the tack room. Trixie raced after him. "Don't be like that, Regan," she begged. "Is there really any chance that the Wheelers are going to keep five horses after this?"

He hummed a few more bars of the tune, then said, "If you can keep secrets from me, Trixie Belden, I guess I can keep one little secret from you."

Trixie's cheeks flamed. "I don't know what you're talking about," she mumbled unhappily.

Regan hummed while Jim and Brian put the three horses in their stalls. When they left the stable, he said in a low voice to Trixie, "No secrets, huh? Miss Trask was telling me about your nightmare, and she also told about Honey and Jim switching rooms." He hummed another bar. "Since when did the early morning sun bother Honey, and since when did you have bad dreams?"

Trixie tossed her head. "All right," she said. "Since when did Jupe go around kicking chauffeurs in the face? If you swallowed that one, I should—"

"Now *I* don't know what *you're* talking about," he interrupted with a chuckle. "Is that how Dick is supposed to have acquired the shiner?"

"That's what he told me," Trixie said. "But I didn't swallow it."

"He was just kidding you," Regan said. "Dick is so scared of horses he wouldn't even put his foot in the tack room for fear a bridle might bite him."

Honey appeared, then, wearing dungarees and a polo shirt. "Come on, Trixie," she said impatiently. "Celia and the cook are having a fit. They want to get through so they can go to the early show. You'd better go eat, too, Regan," she went on. "They want to leave at seven-fifteen."

"I don't know why they can't walk into town once in a while," he said, scrubbing his hands at the tack room sink.

"It only takes twenty minutes to bike in," Trixie said. "If Dick never comes back, you'd better buy bikes for all the help, Regan." She and Honey hurried away and into the house.

"What made you say that?" Honey asked. "Don't you think Dick is coming back?"

"I'd like to know why he left in the first place," Trixie whispered. "As Regan pointed out, people with black eyes don't usually rush in to see big New York specialists."

"I never thought of that," Honey admitted. "I got a black eye when I was hit by a tennis ball at camp one summer. Nobody paid any attention to me. And I was supposed to be delicate in those days."

They joined the others in the dining-room then.

"Just put everything on the table, Celia," Miss Trask was saying. "Then you and Cook run up and dress for the movies. Helen and Marjorie can do the dishes tonight. I'll send them home in a taxi if Regan isn't back in time."

"Thank you, Miss Trask," Celia said. "It isn't often that we can take in the early show." She hurried through the swinging door to the kitchen.

"What I want to know," Mart said, hungrily eyeing the enormous platter of fried chicken, "is why the cook hasn't got a name like everyone else around here." He smiled at Miss Trask. "It's none of my business, but

I'm curious about the private life of the 'feelthy' rich."

Miss Trask smiled back at him. "There's a very simple explanation, Mart. So far, we have never been able to keep a cook long enough for all of us to remember her name."

Honey giggled. "Mother calls them all Rachel although we've had six different ones since Rachel quit. It was Daddy who hit on the idea of calling them all plain 'Cook.' They don't seem to mind, Mart."

"You ought to hire a chef," he said. "Men are more stable than women."

"Will you stop using big words?" Trixie exploded. "It's getting tiresome. Didn't you have anything to read at camp but a dictionary?"

He glared at her. "What was big about that one? Two little syllables. And surely, a famous equestrienne like you must know the definition of *stable* when it's a noun."

"I know both definitions," Trixie informed him. "But why couldn't you have simply said that men are more reliable than women? Not that they are."

Mart appealed to Miss Trask. "How do you like that? She bawls me out for using big words, then suggests that I use one with four syllables instead of two?"

146

Miss Trask chuckled. "Maybe Trixie thinks you should use more familiar words, Mart."

"Nothing could be more familiar to her," Mart said with a grin, "than the word stable. Honey just had to drag her out of one so we could eat."

"Equestrienne," Trixie said suddenly. "Why couldn't you have simply said that I'm a famous horseback rider?"

"Not that you are," Mart returned. "And if I had known that you were familiar with the word, I would never have applied it to you."

"I give up," Trixie groaned. "Let's eat."

After dinner, they cleared the table, and Brian and Mart insisted upon helping the maids with the dishes.

"We're experts," Mart said, tying a ruffled apron on over his jeans. "Human dishwashing machines. That's the kind of camp we went to."

Brian vigorously scrubbed the huge copper frying pan. "I can make people stop using that old saying about the pot calling the kettle black," he said. "If I could be everywhere at once, there would be no such thing as a black kettle."

"Go along with you," plump Helen said, giggling. "Marjorie and I can do better without you big boys crowding around the sinks."

"That we can," Marjorie agreed, snatching her apron off Mart. "But we thank you kindly just the same."

Mart bowed. "Say no more. We can take a hint. We know when we're not wanted." He and Brian stalked out the back door, pretending to be very hurt.

"Oh, dear," Marjorie said contritely to the girls. "Tell them we're sorry, won't you? We thought it was real nice of them to offer to help."

"Pay them no mind," Trixie said airily. "They had junior counselor jobs this summer, and they haven't recovered yet."

She and Honey followed the boys who were waiting for them outside the kitchen door. In a few minutes, Jim joined them. "I'm so full of food I can hardly walk, let alone ride horseback," he said as they strolled toward the stable.

"Me, too," the others chorused.

"I really ought to go home and get that diamond," Trixie said, and explained to Jim and Brian. "Do you think it's safe in my sewing basket?" she finished.

"Gosh, I don't know," Brian replied worriedly. "Did you say, Mart, that the pincushion showed signs of having been manhandled by Bobby?"

Mart nodded. "Anything stuffed, whether it be in

the form of fruit or wild beast, sooner or later loses its stuffing if Bobby has anything to do with it. The strawberry pincushion bore his mark—a hole in the head."

"Not that strawberries have heads," Trixie said. "But we get the idea, professor. What are you leading up to, Brian?"

"Just this," he said. "If the pincushion bears Bobby's mark, it may mean that he knows it belongs to you. He may well have gouged a hole in it, sometime or other, to pay you back for something you did to him."

"Gleeps," Mart howled. "I should have thought of that. I know that age group only too well. They're uncivilized little savages. Especially when seeking revenge upon older persons; and more especially, poor, hardworking, well-meaning junior counselors. Take my knapsack, for instance—"

"Never mind, never mind," Trixie interrupted. "Just run along and put the diamond in some other, *safer,* place. We'll wait right here for you. In fact, I think I'll curl up on the saddle blankets and take a nap while you're gone."

"Is that so?" Mart grabbed one of her short, sandy curls and gave it a gentle yank. "If you're so smart, you can go and retrieve the diamond yourself."

"Better not stand around arguing about it," Brian

advised them. "Bobby's favorite time for committing vandalism, I seem to remember, is after he's supposed to be tucked safely in bed." He pointed to the clock on the tack room wall. "It's almost eight."

"You're *so* right," Trixie moaned. "We may already be too late. Come on, Mart, please come with me. I couldn't stand it alone if that diamond has disappeared again."

Chapter 12
Mr. Lytell's Observations

Mart and Trixie raced into their house and up the stairs to the attic. Mrs. Belden called to them from the hall below before they had a chance to pick their way across the boxes and trunks to the spot where they hoped the sewing basket would be.

"Is that you, Trixie?" she asked. "Did you come back for something?"

"And how!" Mart muttered under his breath. "It's Mart and Trixie, Moms," he called from the top step.

"All right," she said. "Having a good time?"

"Wonderful," Trixie replied. "You were an angel to give me a vacation, Moms."

"You deserved it," Mrs. Belden said.

They heard her go down the stairs to the ground floor, and then they hurried over to a corner under the eaves.

"Eureka!" Mart chortled. "It's here."

"The pincushion," Trixie said weakly. "You look, Mart."

"It's here, too," he said. "And so is the diamond. Bobby should sue us for libel."

Trixie cuddled the precious stone in her hand for a minute, then she crammed it back inside the strawberry pincushion. "Now what, Mart?"

"If you could only sew," he said, "you could sew the thing right inside the pincushion and substitute it for the one Moms has just like it in her sewing basket. It would be perfectly safe there, even from Bobby. He never touches her things."

"I can't sew well enough to make this strawberry look just like the one Moms has," Trixie admitted. "But Honey could. She's expert with any kind of needle, and, after all, there's only just a rip in the seam." She scrabbled through the basket and finally found some red thread which exactly matched the strawberry.

"You'll need a needle, too," Mart reminded her, "or do you know that much about mending?"

Trixie giggled. "Don't needle me. Let's go. And let's appoint Brian a committee of one to do the substituting. Moms and Dad would never suspect him of doing anything peculiar. He's the fair-haired boy around here, even if he is a brunet."

"Wait a sec," Mart cautioned her. "You can't go barging downstairs with anything as suspicious as sewing equipment in your hand. Moms would faint with surprise. Besides, we ought to be carrying something which would explain why we came back."

Trixie sighed and crammed the pincushion, thread, and a package of needles into the pocket of her jeans. "What might we need that Moms didn't pack?" She stared around the cluttered floor.

"Certainly not Bobby's old high chair or play pen," Mart said in a discouraged tone of voice, "or his crib. Say, why don't they keep kids that age in cribs anyway? Cribs with ceiling-high iron bars?"

"Write a letter to your congressman about it," Trixie said with a giggle. "I've got it," she cried suddenly. "Those old roller skates. Jim has been promising to make Bobby a scooter out of an orange crate for ages. We'll each carry a pair. Come on."

Trixie hurried down the steep stairs so fast that she tripped on the bottom step and fell headlong into the hall. As she scrambled up, Bobby appeared at his bedroom door.

"Hey!" he greeted them. "Whatcha gonna do with those roller skates?"

"A scooter for you," Trixie said sweetly. "Jim's going to make you one. Now go to bed, Bobby."

Suddenly he burst into tears. "Oh, oh, and I was such a bad boy. Trixie," he wailed, "I choppeded Dinah's head off."

Trixie knelt and pulled him into her arms. "It doesn't matter, Bobby, darling," she crooned. "Dinah is just an old rag doll. I should have given her to you long ago. Anyway, I was a bad girl to mess up your toy box."

"She certainly was," Mart said soothingly. "And I'm a bad boy not to have made you a scooter before I went to camp." He took Bobby back to bed and together they tucked him in.

All smiles now, he kissed them good night and they hurried away. Mr. Belden stopped them in the downstairs hall, eyeing the roller skates. "So Bobby's going to have a scooter at last?"

"That's right, Dad," Mart said. "I'm really terrible. Jim is a better big brother to Bobby than Brian and I are."

"I wouldn't say that," his father said, chuckling. "In fact, when you're home, you and Brian spoil the child to death."

"He can't accuse me of that," Trixie said, later, when she and Mart were climbing the hill. "I'm the terrible one. I'm forever losing my temper when I have to take care of Bobby, and he really is so cute."

"Oh, well," Mart said cheerfully, "you'll improve with age. In fact, according to Moms and Dad, you've taken great strides this summer. I have a feeling that Honey has a good influence on you. She's really super."

"I *love* her," Trixie cried. "She's got just about everything, and I don't mean money."

"Money," Mart said airily. "Oh, that! Say, Jim's great, too. Brian thinks the world of him already. He hopes they'll be in the same class at High."

"I hope so, too," Trixie said and led the way into the tack room. She gave Honey the thread, needles, and pincushion while Mart explained.

"You're to make the switch, Brian, old boy, old boy," Mart finished. "Trixie and I have had too many narrow escapes already." He wiped his moist brow on the sleeve of his shirt. "Whew! Suppose Dad had caught Trixie with that mending gear in her hand! Bro-*ther,* would he ever have been suspicious."

Honey quickly and deftly repaired the ripped seam and handed the pincushion to Brian. "It all comes of being the eldest son," she said, smiling. "Are you going to slip this into your mother's sewing basket now, or in the dead of the night?"

Brian groaned. "In the dead of the night, I hope to be on hand to help catch our prowler." He glared at Mart. "If you think Dad's suspicions would have been aroused if he had caught Trixie with this feminine object, what's he going to think if he catches *me* with it?"

"If he does," Mart said cheerfully, "just nibble on it.

In Alaska, strawberries do grow to that size."

"That's a big help," Brian said sarcastically. "Why don't you fly up to Juneau and get me a parka, so I can sneak into the house disguised as an Eskimo?"

"The least we can do," Honey said after Brian had left, "is to have his horse saddled and bridled when he gets back. I'll do it."

"Who's going to ride whom?" Mart said.

"I dibs Susie," Trixie said. "Okay, Honey?"

Honey nodded. "Do you want to ride Strawberry, Mart? I like Lady, especially when I'm tired and sleepy, as I am now." She turned to Jim. "Did Brian get on well with Starlight?"

"They're crazy about each other," Jim said. "Sure you don't want to ride Jupe, Mart?"

"Not me," Mart said. "I'm not good enough. He might black my eye."

"That whole yarn is fishy," Jim said as they saddled and bridled the horses. "I wonder why Dick didn't come back this afternoon?"

"If he doesn't come back tonight," Trixie said, "we won't catch anything in our trap. I've a good mind to take some pills, so I'll be sure to stay awake. Coffee wasn't much help."

"Great," Mart said. "Sweets for the sweet and dope

for the dopes. Give me that saddle, Honey. I'll get Starlight ready for Brian."

Brian himself appeared then. "Nothing to it," he said happily. "Nothing to it. Moms and Dad were upstairs putting Bobby back on top of the bed from his nest under it." He gave Honey his mother's pincushion. "You'd better keep this. You're the only one of us who seems to have a rightful claim to such objects."

"It is exactly like the other one," Honey said, cramming it into the pocket of her jeans. "Have you ever thought of what might happen, Brian, when your mother tries to stick a needle into the one that's half-filled with the diamond?"

"That can't happen," Trixie said firmly. "It just can't. Besides, Moms has one of her knitting fevers on now; and most of the day she's canning tomatoes. I doubt if she'll even look in her sewing basket until she's finished Bobby's sweater."

They mounted their horses and, with Jim and Honey leading the way, started along the trail that led through the woods. "I hope you're right," Mart said to Trixie. "Let's pray that Bobby doesn't yank all the straps off his sunsuits between now and Sunday."

"Do you think the mystery will be solved by then?" Trixie asked.

"I think our prowler will come back," he said, "if that's what you mean."

"And," Brian added, "if we haven't solved the mystery by the time the house party ends, we'll have to give the diamond to the police and confess our sins."

"I suppose so," Trixie said mournfully. "I'd like to know where Dick is now."

The trail ended at a quiet country lane which paralleled Glen Road on the other side of the woods. The Beldens galloped up to join Jim and Honey who had reined in their horses.

"When you have your driving lesson," Honey was telling Jim, "this is where Dick will take you. There's almost no traffic on it, and there's just that one farmhouse over there at the dead end of the road."

"That's right," Brian agreed. "At school the instructors took us out here for steering practice as soon as we knew how to shift gears." He turned to Jim. "Say, that's an idea. If Dick doesn't come back tonight, I can show you the gear-shifting part of the course. There's nothing to it, really."

"Swell," Jim said. "I do want to get the hang of it all as soon as possible."

"How did it happen you never were exposed to the art of driving before?" Mart asked. "When I was ten I started plaguing Dad with questions until I got the general idea, and so did Brian."

"My dad," Jim said in a low voice, "my *own* dad, died when I was ten."

Honey laid her hand lightly on his tanned arm. "Jim had a very mean stepfather, Mart," she said softly. "He wasn't the kind who answers boys' questions about gear-shifting."

Mart's face reddened with embarrassment. "Golly, Jim, I'm sorry," he mumbled. "That was a dumb question I asked you. But then, I'm dumb."

Jim turned around in the saddle to grin at him. "You're anything but that, Mart, and there's no reason for you to apologize. I'm too sensitive. Plenty of boys have had much worse breaks than I had, and very few of them could hope for the good luck of being adopted by such swell people as the Wheelers."

"Oh, Jim," Honey cried gently. "We were the lucky ones. I was the most miserable person in the world until I met you and Trixie."

He tapped her lightly on the cheek. "Don't correct your elders, little sister."

"Oh, woe," Trixie interrupted. "Here comes that nosy Mr. Lytell. Let's gallop off in all directions."

"What's eating you, Trixie?" Brian demanded. "He's

a perfectly harmless character, and I'd like to say hello. You know, of course," he said to Jim and Honey, "that yon man on the sway-backed gray mare owns the little Glen Road store?"

"That we do," Jim said emphatically. "In the days when I was a fugitive from my stepfather, he gave us some bad moments."

"Trixie's right," Honey added. "He's a nosy old gossip, but we've got to be polite. If it weren't for him, we wouldn't get the Sunday papers; and Regan would quit if he couldn't relax over the comics." She raised her voice and said pleasantly, "Good evening, Mr. Lytell. How is Belle bearing up during this hot, sultry weather?"

Mr. Lytell poked at his glasses with one hand and patted the mare's gaunt shoulder with the other. "She can hardly stand it," he told Honey. "But I always say, no matter how old a horse is, it should always have some exercise." He nearsightedly peered at Brian and Mart. "Why, hello, boys. Back from camp, eh?"

"That's right," Brian said. "Did you have a nice summer, sir?"

Belle stumbled to a stop on the other side of the country road, and hung her head dejectedly. "Well, yes and no," Mr. Lytell answered Brian. "It's been so hot

Belle and I only ride early in the morning or late in the evening." He gave Honey and Jim a sharp glance. "You kids been camping out in that old caretaker's cottage on the edge of your property?"

"Why, no," Honey said. "What made you think so?"

"Saw lights flickering in there Tuesday night," he said. "Any of you kids drive cars?"

"I can drive," Brian said, "but I'm not old enough, yet, to get a license. Why?"

"I was just wondering," the old storekeeper said. "Saw a jalopy parked by the road near your cottage, Honey, that same night. And then, early Wednesday morning, I saw it drive away."

"That's interesting," Trixie put in. "When you saw it leave Wednesday morning, Mr. Lytell, were there two men in the car or one?"

He stared at her suspiciously. "Who said there were any men in the car at all?"

Trixie laughed airily. "I never heard of a car driving off by itself before, Mr. Lytell. And it's obvious that someone who had engine trouble was forced to spend Tuesday night in the cottage."

"It isn't obvious at all," he said sourly. "A person with engine trouble—a *decent* person—would have gone up to the big house and asked permission to stay in the cottage until it was light enough to repair the engine."

"You forget, Mr. Lytell," Brian said quietly, "from the road, no one would have the vaguest idea that the cottage belonged to the Wheeler estate. If you can see it at all, it looks as though it's just an abandoned shack in the woods."

"I'm surprised *you* knew it was there," Jim added.

A pale flush spread up over Mr. Lytell's prominent cheekbones. "I notice things," he mumbled. "And I happened to notice that there was only one person in the car when it drove away early Wednesday morning. And, if you kids weren't camping out in the cottage Tuesday night, that person must talk to himself." He picked up the reins and nudged the old horse into a walk. "Belle and I heard voices when we rode by there just as it was getting really dark. Loud voices."

No one said a word until he disappeared from view. Then Trixie said triumphantly, "It's beginning to look as though my theory wasn't so dumb. Loud voices means quarreling."

"But, Trixie," Honey pointed out, "your theory was that both men drove away after the fight." Suddenly she turned white. "Oh, I get it. The *body* of the other man was in the trunk of the jalopy."

163

"Let's leave corpses out of this," Brian said sternly. He shook his finger at Trixie. "We'll all have nightmares."

"I never brought corpses into it," Trixie told him tartly. "Take your stubby finger and shake it at Honey. My latest theory is that one of the men was knocked out during the fight. When he came to, his pal had already left in the car, so he had to hitchhike his way to wherever they were going."

"You know," Mart said thoughtfully, "it does sound like someone double-crossed his buddy and realized too late that he had departed without the loot."

"It doesn't make sense to me," Brian retorted. "If you had something I wanted, I'd knock you out and *take* it from you before I departed."

"Oh, for Pete's sake," Trixie interrupted. "Don't be idiots. Don't you realize that the diamond was only part of the loot? I think the two men had just robbed a safe or something. They got to quarreling when they started to divvy up what they had stolen. That's when the diamond got ground into the mud floor of the cottage."

"I see what you mean," Honey said. "The diamond was probably in a ring and fell out of the setting during the fight. It looks like the kind of stone that belongs in an engagement ring." She frowned. "But then it wouldn't have been in a safe, Trixie. Ladies usually wear their engagement rings all the time, no matter how valuable the stone may be."

Trixie sighed. "Your mother wears hers all the time, but ours doesn't. Before she works in the garden she always takes it off. Anyway," Trixie continued, "Mr. Rubber Heels knocked his partner out and drove away with the loot. Later he discovered that the diamond wasn't in the setting of the ring; so he drove back to the cottage."

Honey nodded. "The second set of tire treadmarks and footprints on the shoulder of the road prove that part of your theory, Trixie. What you're leading up to, I suppose, is that when Rubber Heels came back, his partner had left the cottage; and you and I had already found the diamond."

"That makes some sense," Jim admitted. "Naturally, the double-crosser had no way of knowing whether or not his buddy was still in the cottage. So he sneaked up to the thicket, and when he heard your voices he hid there and soon found out exactly where Honey had put the diamond."

Brian nodded. "So he lurked in the woods near the house all day, and realized that he couldn't possibly sneak in during the day with so many servants on the premises. Thursday night he did sneak in, but Trixie's yell frightened him away."

"You're off your trolley," Trixie broke in. "In the first place, if he spent his time lurking in the woods, he couldn't have found out which room was Honey's. And, in the second place, a perfect stranger couldn't possibly have sneaked into the house Thursday night without Patch barking his head off. I keep telling you," she finished, "Dick's our man."

"She's right," Honey cried. "He lurked in the woods on Wednesday and heard us all talking about how much we needed a chauffeur. So he simply went back to the place where he had left the car and drove up to the garage on Wednesday evening to apply for the job, hoping that he'd be given a room on the third floor."

"Fine," Jim jeered. "Great. How did he get the letter of recommendation from Mr. Whitney?"

Trixie sighed. "I wish you'd never seen that letter, Jim. It ruins everything." She straightened suddenly. "Maybe it was forged!"

"Listen, Trixie," Jim said with a sigh. "It takes time and practice to make a perfect copy of another person's signature. Especially if you don't know who the person is and have no way of getting a sample of his signature."

Honey giggled. "He's right, Trixie," she said. "How could Dick have known that Mr. Whitney was a friend of Daddy's? And, even if he did, how could he have got hold of something with Mr. Whitney's signature on it to copy from? He produced that letter of recommendation the morning after we found the diamond."

"I can't answer any of those questions," Trixie admitted. "Let's ride. If we don't give these horses some exercise, Regan will be awfully, awfully surprised. He's suspicious enough, as it is."

Chapter 13
Bob-Whites of the Glen

It was dark when they finished grooming their horses. Regan came back from the village, then, with Celia and the cook in the Ford.

He put the car in the garage and called up the stairs. "Dick! You back?"

No answer. "Well, I like that," he grumbled. "For two cents I'd black his other eye. Tomorrow morning I'll have to go in for Helen and Marjorie, and, most likely, drive them home again."

"It's a shame," Honey said sympathetically. "I'll ask Miss Trask if they can take a taxi until Dick does come back."

"No, don't do that," Regan said. "Taxis, taxis! Rich as your dad is, Honey, I can't stand it. It's too extravagant." He grinned at them. "As long as you kids help me with the horses, I'll make out all right."

"Oh, we will," Trixie assured him. "I'll make sure that Susie is exercised and groomed and everything every day." She moved closer to him. "Ah, please, Regan, tell me the secret."

"Scat, all of you," he said, pretending to be very stern. "Next thing you know, Miss Trask will fire me for making you do my work!" Humming cheerfully, he climbed the stairs to his room.

"Let's raid the icebox," Jim said, staring up at the third-floor windows. "Celia and the cook have retired for the night. And I trust, Nailor, too."

"He's probably hiding in one of the empty guest rooms," Trixie said. "Just waiting until we all go to bed. Then," she added in an ominous whisper, "he'll sneak into your room, Jim, chloroform you, and—"

"Stop it," Honey begged, shivering. "Do you really suspect Nailor again, Trixie?"

"No, I don't," she said, laughing. They all trooped into the kitchen. Jim hooked the screen door.

"Why don't you suspect him?" Honey asked. "You did once."

"I didn't know he was such a well-known character in the village, then," Trixie said, accepting the bottle of cold soda Jim handed her. "Besides, he couldn't sneak around the house without arousing Patch. The dogs don't like him. They growl at him whenever he comes near them, and the hackles rise on Reddy's neck when he tries to pet him."

"That's hard to believe," Mart said. "Why, Reddy is

such a dope he'd lead a burglar right to the place where you keep the family silver, Honey."

"A burglar, yes; but Nailor, no," Trixie said. "Like Mr. Lytell, I notice little things like that. And the dogs adore Dick. They positively fawn on him. It's disgusting. All because he bought them some bones in the village."

"Speaking of which," Jim said to Honey, "did you get the mail today? I expected a book on how to train pointers."

"Oh, I forgot," Honey gasped. "It was my turn, wasn't it?" She grabbed Trixie's hand. "Run down to the mailbox with me, won't you? I'm scared to go way down to the road alone now that it's dark."

"Skip it," Jim said. "Miss Trask probably got the mail. She usually does before dinner if we forget."

"Before dinner?" Brian asked. "That mailman is a regular diller-dollar, ten o'clock scholar. He used to arrive in the morning; then it was changed to late afternoon, and now it's in the evening?"

"He still brings the mail, with *The Sleepyside Sun,* around five," Trixie told him. "Honey and Jim are supposed to take turns getting it, but Honey never remembers. When she forgets, Miss Trask goes down to the box for it just before dinner."

"I'll bet she didn't today," Honey said. "She was

awfully busy. I'll go down now, Jim, if Trixie will come with me."

Jim grinned. "All right, it might teach you to remember. It just might. Here's a flashlight." He unlatched the door for them.

The girls hurried down the driveway to the mail-box at the foot of the hill. Honey yanked it open. "My stars," she said. "It's full of mail. Miss Trask was too busy, for once. And I guess this is the book Jim was waiting for."

They raced back up the hill and dumped the letters and packages on the kitchen table. "Ah, my book," Jim cried. "This will keep me awake all night."

"Is there anything there that'll keep us awake, Honey?" Trixie asked. "I just know Dick is going to come sneaking back at midnight."

Miss Trask called, then, from the top of the back stairs. "It's time you were all in bed. Come on up now. Leave that light burning over the sink, Jim; but turn out the others."

"Okay," Jim said. "Is Patch up there with you, Miss Trask?"

"No," she said. "I haven't seen him since you fed him."

Jim whistled a few times, and then they heard the

puppy scratching and whining on the other side of the screen door. When Jim opened the door, Patch bounded in, slipped on the waxed linoleum, and skidded across the floor.

"He's just like Reddy," Trixie said, laughing. "Reddy does that every time. Is he going to sleep in your room tonight, Jim?"

"No, he sleeps on the porch," Jim said. "It almost completely encircles the house, you know; so if any stranger tried to get in through the doors or windows, Patch would hear him."

"Hm," Trixie said thoughtfully as they trooped upstairs. Later, when she and Honey were in bed she said, "Jim must know that our prowler wasn't a stranger. Whom does he suspect?"

"I really don't know," Honey said sleepily. "As you keep saying, Patch would have barked his head off if any stranger had tried to get in the house last night. But I know Jim doesn't suspect Dick. On account of that letter from Mr. Whitney, you know."

"I've been thinking about that," Trixie said. "It was your turn to get the mail on Wednesday, wasn't it?"

"Uh-huh," Honey murmured.

"Did you get it?" Trixie asked.

But Honey was sound asleep. In a few minutes, try

as she did to stay awake, Trixie, herself, was sound asleep. When she awoke, it was morning, a steaming hot morning with the threat of rain hanging heavy in the air. She and Honey put on bathing suits and, as had been pre-arranged, met the boys down at the boathouse.

"Did anything happen last night?" they asked Jim in one breath.

"Not a thing," he said, "except that Dick hasn't come back yet. And is Regan furious!"

"Regan," Brian explained, "was already in the lake when we got down here. Trying to cool off in more ways than one. He just went up to get dressed. He's got to go in for the maids and the laundress."

They swam out to the raft, and then Honey said, "Dick is going to be fired as soon as Daddy gets back. If you think Regan is angry, think what kind of a mood Daddy would be in if he knew the new chauffeur was AWOL so soon after being hired."

"And all on account of one little back eye," Mart added. "What a sissy that guy must be."

"Don't be silly," Trixie said, shaking water out of her ear by hopping up and down on the raft. "Dick didn't go off on account of his black eye. He went off for some other reason, and it has something to do with the mystery."

"What, exactly?" Mart demanded. "Elucidate, my dear Holmes."

She whirled on him, and he pretended to cringe with fright. "I take elucidate back," he howled. "I take it all back. What I meant was, explain, make clear your statement, Miss Belden."

Trixie giggled. "I can't explain, make clear, or elucidate. I just feel it in my bones."

Mart groaned. "Feminine intuition. Gleeps, noodlehead, spare us that."

"I'll spare you that and a lot more," Trixie said tartly. "I was just going to explain, make clear, and elucidate to you about the letter of recommendation from Mr. Whitney. But since I'm a noodlehead, I'd better keep it to myself."

"I modify that statement," Mart said promptly. "You're not a noodlehead; you're merely equipped with scrambled brains."

"Scrambled eggs would be nice now," Jim said with a grin. "And here come Miss Trask and Celia with the wherewithal." He dove off the float and, with his fast crawl, struck cleanly through the water toward the boathouse.

They all followed him and a few minutes later were busy preparing breakfast. With everyone helping, they soon had a feast spread out on the table on the boathouse porch.

"Honey," Mart said approvingly, "is hereby elected chief waffle-maker of the club." He waved a skewer at Trixie. "And you, addlebrain, are the barbecue chef."

"I told you Honey and I are marvelous cooks," Trixie said smugly.

"Oh, let's do have a club," Honey interrupted. "When I was in boarding school, I was always reading books about boys and girls who were members of secret clubs and had *such* fun." She added wistfully, "I never thought the day would come when I might belong to one."

"The Riders of the Glen, that's what we are," Mart yelled excitedly. "R.O.G. We'll call ourselves the Rogues."

"Speak for yourself, knave," Brian said with a chuckle. "Just because you're a rascal doesn't mean the rest of us are."

"Couldn't we be sort of Robin Hoods or something like that?" Honey asked. "The name of the red trailer was the *Robin,* you know. And the Darnells were the kind of people Robin Hood would have helped in olden times."

"We're better at riding than we are at archery," Mart objected.

"And we think of ourselves as detectives," Jim

added, grinning, "although we didn't prove much last night."

" 'If at first you don't succeed, try, try again,' " Trixie chanted. "Canadian mounties are sort of detectives on horseback. And, in a way, they're modern Robin Hoods. Their motto isn't simply 'get your man.' They are trained to give help to anyone who needs it."

"How educated can we get?" Mart asked. "Where did you pick up that knowledge, Trix?"

"In a book," she informed him airily. "Just because I can't thread a needle doesn't mean I can't read."

"You've got an idea," Honey said. "We can't be *Canadian* mounties, but when we have secret meetings we could wear special red jackets which I can make easily. We might call ourselves the Glen Road Robins, and we could have the cottage for our clubhouse."

"Swell," Jim put in. "Brian, Mart, and I can fix the roof and put new panes of glass in the windows. But let's not be robins, let's be bobwhites." He whistled. "Bob*white*. Bob*white*. Remember, girls, that was our signal when I was hiding from Jonesy."

"That's right," Trixie cried. "And don't they flock together in little groups called bevies? Instead of having a meeting, we could have a bevy, which would be more mysterious."

"Bobwhites are quails," Mart said, chortling. "And I quail with surprise every time Trixie says something that makes sense." He turned to Honey. "Bob is sort of a nickname for Robin. Are you happy about the whole thing?"

"Oh, yes," Honey said. "Bob-Whites of the Glen! B.W.G. Nobody could ever guess what those initials stood for. I can cross-stitch them in white on the back of our red shirts."

"A motto," Brian said. "We should have a motto!"

"How about thinking of ourselves as one big family?" Honey asked. "I mean, we're all brothers and sisters, and if one of us is ever in need, we'll never fail him or her?"

"I like that a lot," Jim said slowly. "If all the world had the same motto, there'd never be any wars."

"I'm all for it," Brian said. "Mart and I could use another brother like you, Jim, and another sister like you, Honey."

"I agree for the same reasons," Mart said, his blue eyes twinkling. "Honey and Trix sort of cancel each other out, so it makes it almost bearable having a sister. That's how *I* feel."

Trixie tossed her sandy curls as she stacked the paper plates. "If you're stuck with three brothers you might as well have one more. And Honey and I have felt like sisters ever since we first met, haven't we, Honey?"

Honey nodded, her hazel eyes filmed with tears of happiness. "It's all like a dream coming true. I can't believe it! A secret club and—well, just everything I always wanted."

When they had cleaned up the boathouse, Jim said, "The first favor I'm going to ask of my new brother, Brian, is a driving lesson. How about it?"

"Swell," Brian said. "If you haven't mastered the art of gear-shifting in an hour, I'll chew Honey's bathing cap and blow bubbles with it." They hurried off up the path toward the garage.

Mart stretched lazily. "Why do you suppose no one walked into our trap last night?" he asked. "From what I know about Jim, he would have been wide awake if anyone had dropped a pin on the hall carpet outside the room. He's so used to taking care of himself, he's acquired the protective instincts of woods animals."

Honey smiled. "Anyway, the alertness of them. No, if Jim heard nothing, no one tried to get into my old room last night."

"Of course, he didn't," Trixie said, leading the way up the hill. "I mean, Dick didn't, because he wasn't here, but here he comes now. That's his car, anyway."

They stared at the green jalopy that was rattling along the driveway. It stopped near the garage and Dick got out.

Trixie nudged Honey. "His black eye is better, but he's got the prettiest attack of poison ivy I've ever seen!"

Chapter 14
"Leaflets Three"

"Oh, oh," Honey cried in a low voice. "I know what you mean, Trixie. If anyone was lurking around in the woods on Wednesday, he'd be sure to have a rash from the poison ivy by now."

"Not necessarily," Mart said. "Not unless he's allergic. I'm not, for one. But our friend, Dick, obviously is. Bobby had better give him lessons on 'leaflets three, let it be.' " He chuckled. "If Trixie were not here, I would have said, avoid trifoliolate leaves. They may contain an irritating substance called urushiol."

"Now, you're talking like Brian, the medical man," Trixie moaned.

"Exactly," Mart said. " 'Twas Brian who taught me that lingo. I tried to pass it along to the small fry at camp, but, no, even 'leaflets three' was over their dear little heads."

"I'd better go ask Miss Trask for some calamine lotion for Dick," Honey said. "The side of his face where he hasn't the black eye might swell up like anything. It looks puffy, right now."

Regan came out of the garage and gave Dick one look. "For Pete's sake," he said with a sigh. "Now what? You'd better go right back to your doc, Dick, and get some medicine. That rash on your face and hands is going to get a lot worse before it gets better."

"Forget it," Dick growled. "I've had poison ivy before. It's nothing to get excited about."

Regan's sandy eyebrows shot up. "But a black eye is, huh? Well, well. I learn something every day. Where did you get the shiner, fella?"

"Jupe kicked him," Trixie said impudently. "And Jupe's hoof was contaminated because he had been galloping through the woods. It explains everything—even the poison ivy."

Dick whirled to glare at her. "Fresh as paint, aren't you? Why don't you go home where you belong?"

"Take it easy, Dick," Mart said, obviously controlling his temper with an effort. "It so happens that we Beldens were invited to spend the weekend up here."

"It so happens," Regan went on hotly, "that the Beldens have been invited to spend all their spare time up here. If you, Dick, spent a little of your spare, or otherwise, time around here, it would help." He pointed toward the station wagon which was parked between the garage and the stable. "Brian is giving Jim a lesson in gear-shifting at the moment. I got the impression that *that* was your job."

Immediately, the disagreeable expression on Dick's face faded. "Gee, I'm sorry about that," he said, almost contritely. "Jim's a good kid. I'll give him a driving lesson right away."

"Oh, no, you won't," Regan corrected him. "You'll get right into uniform. Miss Trask is about ready to go in and do the weekend shopping. When you get back, it'll be time to take Winnie, the laundress, home. Then you can have lunch. After that you can drive Helen home. She has the afternoon off. When you get back from that, it'll be time to take Marjorie in to town. She's getting off early today, because she worked overtime last night." He put his big freckled hands on his hips. "Between then and dinnertime you can give Jim a lesson, *if* you've cleaned the cars. The sedan could stand a coat of wax."

Dick placed his own thin hands on his hips, frowning. "And what, may I ask, are *you* going to be doing all day?"

"Me?" Regan's eyes were very green. "I'm going to clean out the stable, that's all. And tonight I'm going to watch the wrestling matches on television." He chuckled wryly. "I'd invite you to join me, but you're going to

be too busy. And if you don't take care of that poison ivy, you won't be able to see by then, anyway." He strode off into the stable.

"What's eating him, Miss Honey?" Dick asked, in a bewildered voice.

Miss Honey to her, Trixie thought, *because she's the boss's daughter. But I'm fresh as paint.*

As though reading her mind, Honey said quickly, "Please don't call me miss, Dick. And Regan is cross because he had to do a lot of driving last evening and this morning. He hates it, you know. Cares about nothing but the horses." She came closer and stared at the rash on his face. "You'd better take his advice, Dick. If that rash spreads, both of your eyes may close. Why don't you see our doctor when you take Miss Trask into the village? He'll give you some pills and a salve. I'll go in now, and make an appointment for you, if you like. Miss Trask will be shopping for hours, and she won't need you, except when she's through, so you can carry the cartons from the super market to the car."

"That's very nice of you," he said, "but I won't bother, thanks. If she's going to spend a lot of time in the village, I'll come back out here and give the sedan a coat of wax. Then I'll be free to give Jim a driving lesson before dinner. I don't like to break my promise to him."

"Well, that's very nice of *you*," Honey said with a quick smile. "Did Miss Trask tell you how to get to the dead-end road on the other side of the woods? It's the safest place for Jim to practice steering if you think he's ready for that this afternoon."

"Sure," Dick said affably. "You go right at the end of Glen Road, then you go right again. I know how to get to that little country lane, all right. No traffic on it, huh?"

"That's right," Mart said. "We call it Hoyt Lane. Mr. Hoyt owns the farm, and his house is the only one on the road. He's busy right now, harvesting, so I doubt if you'll even pass his truck if you and Jim go there this afternoon."

"Fine," Dick said. "And go we will. If your brother is teaching him how to shift gears now, Jim will be ready to get the knack of steering this afternoon. He's a bright boy, Jim is."

"He certainly is," Trixie said, forcing her lips into a smile. "How do you suppose you got that poison ivy, Dick?"

He narrowed his eyes. "If you must know, Miss Nosy, it was taking care of your little brother. Bobby ran into the woods the other day, and I ran after him."

"Oh, my," Trixie said, pretending to be very upset. "Then I guess Bobby has a rash now, too. He's very allergic." She slipped her arm through Honey's. "Well, I'm not going to worry. Moms is armed to the teeth with all sorts of remedies which work like magic."

They strolled off, followed by Mart. "Let's take a look-see at our clubhouse," he said, adding, as soon as they were some distance from the garage, "That guy couldn't speak the truth if it were written out for him in words of one syllable. Ever since Bobby had that bad attack in May, he never goes near anything that remotely resembles poison ivy."

"That's right," Trixie said. "He's even wary of Virginia creeper and wild blackberry vines. If he ran into the woods, it was at a spot where he knows there is no poison ivy."

"I know," Honey said. "He's much smarter than I am. Besides, we've had men out here spraying ever since we bought the place. There's hardly any poison ivy growing now in the woods near the house and the stable and the garage."

"There's plenty right there," Mart said, pointing to the shrubbery at the foot of the lawn. "If we're going to spend a lot of time fooling around the cottage, we'd better try to get rid of it. Trixie hasn't got the brains Bobby has."

"We'll encourage the wild honeysuckle and the wisteria," Trixie said. "They choke out everything. The wisteria, Mart, is what ruined the roof of the cottage. Do you think you boys can fix it so it won't leak?"

Mart went inside the cottage and stared up at the ridgepole. "We'll have to cut away the vines and start all over again," he said. "What I mean is, we can patch up the leaks with heavy tar paper. That stuff is so tough you can use it instead of concrete for making small swimming pools."

"It also costs money," Trixie pointed out. "Where are we going to get the money for repairs?"

"We're going to work for it, of course," Mart said. "How else do you get money, dope?"

"Oh, dear," Honey said. "Trixie is saving every cent she earns so she can buy that colt. Couldn't Jim and I pay her share?"

"No, you couldn't," Mart said. "And I think that, even though you and Jim are loaded with the stuff, you'll have to pretend you're as broke as the other members of the club. 'Rosie O'Grady and the colonel's lady' is the idea. We'll all be brothers and sisters in poverty, or it wouldn't be any fun."

"You're absolutely right, Mart," Honey said quickly. "It was very silly of me to say what I did. How will we earn the money for repairing the clubhouse?"

Mart stared up at the sloping lawns and the flower

beds. "Brian and I are right handy with a lawn mower," he said. "I have a feeling Nailor could be kept busy enough with the flowers so we could pick up some change after school and weekends."

"Of course," Honey cried. "And the vegetable garden. It's full of weeds, and the tomatoes and things are rotting because nobody picks them or anything. Miss Trask would be thrilled to death if you and Brian would take over the lawns, Mart."

"I'll contribute whatever you think is fair from the five dollars a week Dad pays me," Trixie offered.

"Good girl." Mart clapped her affectionately on the shoulder. "And I know how much you want that colt, Trix."

"But what'll *I* do?" Honey wailed. "I can't do anything really well."

"Not much you can't," Mart said. "You sew like a dream. I'll bet Moms would be glad to pay you something just for keeping Bobby in shoulder straps."

"Oh, oh!" Honey's hazel eyes were wide with delight. "Do you really think she would, Mart? It would be so wonderful to *earn* money. You don't know how I've envied Trixie."

"There's nothing like it," Mart agreed. "Now, there's one little hitch. Jim may want the job of mowing the lawns or working in the vegetable garden, or both, and we can't do Nailor out of a job, or can we?"

"Don't worry about Nailor," Honey said hastily. "There's enough to do around here to keep two men like him busy. And as for Jim, I know he's been dying to do something about the vegetable garden, but Gallagher wouldn't let him go near it. Gallagher wouldn't let him mow the lawns or do anything. He was awfully dog-in-the-mangerish about his job, although he didn't do it properly."

"That's the answer, of course," Mart said. "Gallagher was afraid that Jim would show him up. Won't Nailor feel the same way?"

"I don't think so," Honey said. "He hasn't been here quite long enough to feel that he owns the place, the way Gallagher did. Nailor is already complaining about how much work there is. I think he'd be glad if he had nothing to do but putter around with the flowers and shrubs. Heaven knows, there are enough of them; and they almost all need more care than they get."

"That's true," Trixie said. "Even I know that the chrysanthemums should have been pinched back long ago, and as for the delphiniums, Mother would burst into tears if she saw how they've been neglected."

"Why don't you get the job of flower-tending?"

Mart asked. "How green your thumb has grown this summer! Last year you didn't know the difference between forget-me-nots and sunflowers."

Trixie grinned. "I learned the hard way, working for Moms. Boy, she's a slave-driver when it comes to the care of little growing things."

"And your place," Honey said, "is always as neat as a pin. Now that you're back from camp, won't you have to mow your own lawn, Mart?"

He snapped his fingers. "Oh, that! Brian and I can polish it off before breakfast once a week. It's the size of a pincushion compared to yours."

"Don't mention that word," Trixie said with a shudder. "I wish Honey would go right home now and get a mending job from Moms. It might give her an excuse for checking up on the diamond." She giggled and gave Honey a little push. "Go on, and tell Moms you'll take care of everything in her basket. She'll hire you on the spot. Brian and Mart probably brought home a dozen pairs of socks that need darning."

"All right," Honey said soberly. "I love to darn, Trixie."

"Don't be silly," Trixie said. "I was only joking. We don't have to start earning money this weekend, do we, Mart?"

He swung the cottage door back and forth on its rusty hinges. "The sooner we start, the sooner we can turn this ramshackle place into a decent clubhouse."

"True, true," Trixie said impatiently. "But if we want to keep on the good side of Regan, we'd better exercise the horses before it gets too hot. We won't be able to ride this evening; not if we're going to the movies."

"That's right," Honey said. "And Jim must have had enough of gear-shifting by now. Let's all go for a ride and discuss plans for getting our clubhouse into shape."

Up at the stable, they found Jim and Brian waiting for them. "Oh, for the feel of solid reins in my hands again," Jim said ruefully. "And stirrups for my aching feet. I wouldn't be a chauffeur if you paid me."

"We don't want you to get paid for *that*," Mart said, grinning. "How do your aching hands and feet feel about farming on a small scale? A vegetable garden for your very own?"

"Lead me to it," Jim said, brightening. "Anything to get away from the smell of gasoline."

Mart explained while they rode through the woods. "We'll need at least fifteen dollars to make the cottage rainproof," he finished. "There are three of us boys. Do you think Miss Trask would pay us what Dad pays Trix,

Jim? Five dollars a week for keeping the lawns and the vegetable garden out of Nailor's hair?"

"I know she would," Jim said. "It would be worth more than fifteen dollars a week to keep Nailor happy. I think Miss Trask herself would resign if she had to try and find another gardener. And Nailor *is* complaining about the work."

Honey nodded. "I heard him grumbling to Miss Trask this morning. I got the idea that he likes working with the flowers and shrubs but is slightly allergic to lawns and vegetables."

"This job business," Jim said, "is the best idea anyone ever had. I've been on vacation too long now. But, Mart, since you're the one who's going to agricultural college, wouldn't you like to take over the vegetables?"

"But how about you, Jim?" Mart asked. "You spent a lot of your life on a farm, didn't you?"

Jim nodded. "I can also mow lawns. Which job do *you* prefer, Mart?"

"Gee, Jim," Mart cried, "you know I like to grub around with vegetables. My fingers itch to get out there with a hoe and hill up your potatoes."

"Then it's settled," Jim said. "Take your itching fingers to the vegetable garden whenever you feel like it."

"Charity begins at home," Trixie said. "Our own potatoes will need hoeing soon again."

"That's your job," Mart said airily. "I wouldn't think of doing you out of it."

"Thanks," Trixie said. She giggled. "I can't help thinking it's funny. Jim has half a million dollars in stocks and bonds, and yet he's going to mow lawns for five dollars a week."

"It's not funny at all," Jim told her. "You know perfectly well I'm not going to touch a cent of the money I inherited until I'm ready to start my boys' school." He flicked a deer fly from Jupe's glossy, black neck. "And as for Honey, it's great that she's going to have a chance to earn some money."

"I'm so excited I won't be able to thread a needle when the time comes," Honey said. "Do you really think your mother will hire me, Trixie?"

"I'll let you in on a little secret," Trixie said, chuckling. "Moms likes to sew and knit, but she does *not* like to mend. Especially during the canning season. Monday is her birthday. The nicest present Dad could give her would be *you* for the next few weeks. I'm going to call him up and suggest it when we get back."

"Bro*ther!*" Mart yelled. "Monday *is* Moms's birthday. I haven't bought her a thing. Have you, Brian?"

"No," Brian admitted. "But Trixie has a plan. You know how Moms hates to have us spend our hard-earned cash on presents for her."

"That's right," Trixie said. "So, from now until school starts, I thought we'd take turns doing all the cooking. You learned how at camp, and, when I make up my mind to it, I'm not too bad myself."

Mart chortled. "Let's not have broiled tomatoes every meal you cook. Honey must teach you how to make waffles." He patted Trixie's cheek affectionately. "All kidding to one side, Sis, it's a great idea. You can fix breakfast; I'll do lunch, and Brian can cook supper. He does something to spareribs that makes my mouth water. We'll have them every night. They're cheap."

"I wish I could do something like that for my mother," Honey said quietly. "It's so hard to buy her anything, and so silly, too. Whenever she wants anything, she buys it herself."

"I know something you could do for your mother," Trixie said. "Your handwriting is beautiful, and she gets an awful lot of letters from people asking for donations to their pet charities. A lot of the mail we brought up from the mailbox last night looked like appeals for money. You could answer them for her, Honey. Miss Trask couldn't possibly have time to."

"It's a wonderful idea," Honey cried. "I can even draw the checks and have them all ready for her to sign. I know about how much she gives to each charity. Why, I could be sort of a private secretary, couldn't I?"

"That's right," Trixie said. "And you could do the same thing for your father. His own secretary at the office in New York must be pretty busy. Speaking of which," she went on, turning to Jim, "did anybody check up on Dick's letter of recommendation from Mr. Whitney?"

They all stopped their horses in a little clearing in the woods and stared at Trixie. "Why, I don't know what you mean," Jim said. "It was one of those TO WHOM IT MAY CONCERN things. Typewritten. But Dad certainly knows Mr. Whitney's signature when he sees it. They've been corresponding for years. Why should anyone check?"

"I'd like to see that signature," Trixie said mysteriously. "And I'd also like to know, Honey, if your father was expecting a letter from Mr. Whitney which he never got."

Chapter 15
Signatures

Honey stared at Trixie. "What *are* you talking about? What makes you think Daddy was expecting a letter from Mr. Whitney?"

"Well, was he, or wasn't he?" Trixie asked.

"I don't know," Honey said. "Daddy was on vacation, you know, until he was suddenly called to Chicago. His secretary forwarded any letters she couldn't answer herself up here. He *might* have been expecting one from Mr. Whitney which didn't arrive until after he left. But what difference does it make, Trixie? It couldn't have been important. They don't correspond about business. They just write to each other arranging to meet for luncheon or for fishing or hunting trips and things like that."

"I see," Trixie said, turning back to Jim. "Since that letter of recommendation wasn't personal, do you think I could see it? It was just written to 'whom it may concern,' wasn't it?"

"That's right," Jim said. "It was really just the simple kind of reference that most employers give their employees when they're honorably discharged. You know. 'This is to certify that Richard Blank worked for me as a chauffeur for the past three years. I found him honest, industrious, and satisfactory in every way.' So what?"

"So it's all right for me to look at it, isn't it?" Trixie asked.

"Perfectly all right," Jim said, "except that I haven't got it. Dad was in such a hurry when he left Thursday morning, he glanced at it, showed it to me, and then tossed it into a pigeonhole of his desk."

"I dare you to look for it," Trixie said.

"Well, I won't." Jim picked up his reins. "You're suffering from heat exhaustion, Trixie, but you don't know it. Let's go home and take a swim in the lake before lunch."

Trixie leaned from her saddle to grab his arm. "Please look for it, Jim. It may be important."

He glared at her. "It would have to be important. Anytime I go rummaging through the papers in Dad's desk, you'll know I'm crazy with the heat."

Trixie sighed. "I was afraid you'd say that. Just skip it."

No one said anything while they trotted their horses back to the stable. Regan took one look at the girls' hot, perspiring faces and reached for their horses' bridles.

"Slide off and get into swimming clothes," he told them. "I'll groom Lady and Susie."

"Oh, thanks, Regan," Honey said, quickly dismounting. "This must be the hottest day of the summer."

"It only seems that way," he said, "because a thunderstorm is brewing." He glanced up at the puffy white clouds in the blue sky. "The radio was right for once. We'll get rain this evening."

"I hope it doesn't rain this afternoon," Jim said. "I'm looking forward to my steering lesson. Maybe when I do some real driving, all that gear-shifting business will make sense."

Brian laughed. "From the way Jim talks," he said to Regan, "you'd think he wasn't my prize pupil. He'll be driving circles around us in no time."

"He can have my license any time he wants it," Regan said, slipping a halter over Susie's head. "Now that Dick knows a little something of what this job is like, he isn't so crazy about it. But he's bound and determined to give you a driving lesson this afternoon, Jim. While Miss Trask was buying all the food in the village, he came back and polished the sedan. I'll say that for him."

Trixie and Honey hurried into the house to change into bathing suits. "I wonder why Dick is so anxious to give Jim a driving lesson," Trixie said. "You'd think he'd try to get out of anything he could on a hot, muggy day like this."

"I think he really means well," Honey said. "If only he were nicer to you, I'd like him."

"Nothing would make me like him," Trixie said. "I wish I could see that letter from Mr. Whitney."

"But why?" Honey asked.

"Because," Trixie said, "I have a feeling the signature was forged. If you promise not to say anything to the boys, I'll explain. They'll just make fun of me."

"I won't say a word," Honey said, curling up on the window seat beside Trixie. "I'm dying of curiosity."

"It all depends," Trixie began, "on whether or not you went down for the mail at the regular time on Wednesday afternoon."

Honey thought for a minute. "Wednesday. That was the day we found the diamond. Let me see—No, I forgot as usual, Trixie, and the mail stayed in the box all night. I remember now. Miss Trask brought it up the next morning just when we were sitting down to breakfast. That's when Daddy found out he would have to leave for Chicago right away. If I'd remembered to bring up the mail Wednesday afternoon, he and Mother wouldn't have had to rush so with their packing."

"I thought you probably forgot," Trixie said. "Now, don't you see, Honey? If someone was lurking around in the woods that day, he could have seen the mailman put the stuff in the box around five. Since it stayed there all night, he could have sneaked a letter out of the box that evening without anyone seeing him. *A letter from Mr. Whitney.*"

"I still don't understand," Honey said. "Why would anyone steal some of our mail?"

"Signatures," Trixie said. "References have to have signatures. Anyone can rent a typewriter and type out the 'to whom it may concern' part, but to prove anything you have to have a signature."

"Oh, oh," Honey gasped. "In the mailbox was a letter to Daddy from Mr. Whitney! Dick swiped it and copied the signature. Is that what you've been driving at?"

"That's right," Trixie said.

Honey frowned. "But Mr. Whitney doesn't sign his full name when he writes to Dad. He just signs himself 'Whit.' I've seen it on Christmas cards. They're old, old friends."

Trixie slid off the window seat to the floor, groaning. "I never thought of that. I just took it for granted that they did business together." Suddenly she brightened. "Don't they do *any* business together, Honey? I mean, mightn't there have been a contract or something like that which would mean that Mr. Whitney would have to sign his full name?"

Honey thought for a minute. "I don't really know, Trixie. Anyway, do you think Dick would dare swipe a letter? Isn't robbing the mails a federal offense? Would he dare risk getting G-men on his trail just to get a job with us?"

"The job," Trixie said, "isn't the point. He's after the diamond. I'm sure of it. If it's as valuable as you say it is, wouldn't he take a big risk to get it?"

"I guess so," Honey said.

"Anyway," Trixie went on, "Dick probably only borrowed the letter. Just long enough to steam open the envelope and copy the signature. He probably put the letter back in your box on Thursday while Bobby was showing him around the place. And in that case, there should have been a letter from Mr. Whitney in the Thursday mail."

Honey sighed. "I wouldn't know. Jim collected the mail that day and gave Miss Trask all the letters that were for Mother and Daddy. Anyway, Trixie, just forging Mr. Whitney's nickname, 'Whit,' to the reference wouldn't have helped Dick any. Oh, now I remember," she suddenly interrupted herself. "Mr. Whitney and Daddy belong to the same club. Dad's the treasurer, and the dues are paid in August. There could have been a check from Mr. Whitney in Wednesday's mail."

Trixie jumped to her feet. "Where does Miss Trask put your parents' mail, Honey? If we saw the envelope we might be able to tell if the flap had been steamed open."

Honey shook her head. "Miss Trask forwards all their letters right on to their hotel in Chicago. Let's go swimming, Trixie. It's so hot, and I don't see how you're going to prove that Dick is both a forger and a diamond thief."

"If I had a piece of carbon paper and a piece of tracing paper," Trixie said stubbornly, "I could show you how easy it is to become a forger without much practice."

"I have both," Honey said. "In my desk. Come on." She led the way across the hall and pulled down the front of her desk. "There you are. Now what?"

Trixie pointed to a pad of note paper. "Sign your name on the first sheet."

"Madeleine G. Wheeler," Honey wrote with a flourish.

Trixie stared. "Is that your real name?"

"Of course, it is," Honey told her. "I was named for

my mother. Honey is just a nickname, because of the color of my hair."

Trixie slipped a piece of carbon paper between the first and second sheets of the writing tablet, and laid a piece of tracing paper over Honey's signature. Then she carefully traced the name. After that, she tore the second sheet of paper from the pad and showed Honey a faint, but perfect carbon copy of "Madeleine G. Wheeler." Next, Trixie took Honey's fountain pen and carefully inked over every letter of the carbon copy.

Honey gasped. "My stars, you can't tell the original from your copy! Where on earth did you learn that trick, Trixie?"

"Mart taught it to me," Trixie said with a giggle. "Although I don't think his ambition is to become a forger. He read about it in some book. Anyway, according to Jim, your father only glanced at Mr. Whitney's signature on Dick's reference. If he had looked more closely, he might have seen traces of carbon on the signature. Look at my forgery of your name, and you'll see what I mean."

Honey took the sheet of paper to the window. "I do see what you mean," she said after a moment. "The M and the W are sort of blurred."

"Sh-h," Trixie cautioned her as she heard voices out

in the hall. "Here come the boys. Destroy the evidence, or they'll tease me to death."

They carefully crumpled the three sheets of paper containing Honey's signature and crammed them into Jim's scrap basket. Then they hurried out into the hall.

"What were you doing in my room?" Jim demanded suspiciously.

"It was my room until yesterday," Honey reminded him, smiling. "Hurry up and change, boys. We'll only have time for a dip before lunch."

As Trixie tried to dart by him, Mart stopped her. "The cat that swallowed the canary," he said, "couldn't have looked more guilty. What *have* you two been up to?"

"None of your business," Trixie retorted. "Let me go. It's too hot for you to display your brotherly love of me."

Mart snorted. "Remember the motto of our club— just one big, happy family. That means no secrets. The word is written plainly on both of your girlish faces. S-e-c-r-e-t-s!" He gave Trixie a little shake. "Give."

Trixie pulled away from him, but before she could say anything, Jim interrupted. "Something is rustling inside my scrap basket," he said, striding across the room to the desk. "Aha," he went on. "Crumpled paper. Shall we examine it, men?"

"By all means," Mart said. "By all means. They were trespassing, weren't they?"

"Jim Frayne," Honey screamed. "If you look at those papers, I'll—I'll never forgive you."

He shook with laughter. "That does it. I was only teasing before, but now—"

"Now," Brian said, "we had better investigate further." He strode over to the scrap basket and yanked out the ball of tracing paper. He tossed it to Mart who caught it expertly. Trixie made a dive for him, but he tossed it over her head to Jim who passed it along to Brian.

"Stop it," Honey begged. "It's too hot for dodge ball."

"I think you're all as mean as can be," Trixie cried angrily. "Especially Jim, who pretends to be so honorable all over the place. If you were the least bit honorable, you'd let us take those papers and go away."

"What?" Mart demanded. "Are there more of them? The plot thickens. What *were* you doing?"

"Writing poison letters, of course," Trixie said.

"Gleeps," Mart yelled. "I wash my hands of the whole matter!"

Trixie pushed by him. "I'm going downstairs and telephone Dad about Mom's birthday present. If you delay me one more minute, he'll be out to lunch, and he'll probably buy her something in the village. Honey," she added over her shoulder, "keep them from reading those poison letters if it's the last thing you do. We don't want to lose all of our dear, dear brothers."

Chapter 16
The Missing Box

Trixie's father heartily approved of her plan. "I'd be very glad to pay Honey fifty cents an hour for helping your mother with the mending," he said. "Especially now, when she's so busy canning. And it's just the kind of birthday present she likes, Trixie. Thanks for suggesting it."

Trixie hung up and went back to join the others. They greeted her with very dejected expressions.

"Don't tell her," Mart said sadly. "Let her find it out for herself. The girl sleuth needs practice."

"What's eating all of you?" Trixie demanded. "Let's go swimming."

"Oh, Trixie," Honey cried. "Just look around the room. Something's missing."

Trixie's round, blue eyes traveled at once to Honey's dressing table. The jewelry box was gone! "This is too much," she moaned, sinking down on the rug at Mart's feet. "Bobby must have told Dick about the room-switching. He helped you move, remember?"

Jim nodded. "And Bobby also knew that we didn't

move what he called the 'boxlike thing.' He tried to carry it into my old room several times, but we told him firmly that it must stay in here. That's when he discovered the secret compartment, I guess, and put the diamond inside it."

"Well, anyway," Trixie said, "at last you agree with me that Dick is Suspect Number One. And we still have the diamond. But what kind of a trap can we set now?"

Jim shook his head. "We can't be sure that Dick is Suspect Number One, Trixie. Not yet. When Bobby acquires a bit of information he generally spreads it around fast. He could have told any number of people by now that Honey and I switched rooms."

"I hope you didn't tell him it was a 'see-crud,' " Trixie said forlornly. "If you did, you might just as well have printed the news on the front page of the *Sun.*"

"I did tell him it was a secret," Honey admitted miserably. "It was awfully dumb of me."

"It doesn't make any difference," Trixie said, trying to cheer her up. "Bobby would have told the world about it, anyway. The point is that our prowler must have made up his mind that it would be too risky," she went on, "to try and get the diamond while Jim was sleeping in this room. It would be less of a risk to try and steal the box during the day."

"That's right," Honey agreed. "And today is the day. Winnie, the laundress, always leaves before noon. Helen had the afternoon off, so she left right after that. Marjorie got off early because she worked late last night. Once Nailor leaves the house in the morning, he never comes back except for meals. Celia and the cook have been busy preparing lunch for the past hour. Miss Trask has been in the kitchen putting away the stuff she bought ever since she came back from the village." Honey shrugged. "The whole upstairs has been empty ever since about eleven-thirty. Anyone could have sneaked in through one of the side doors, walked calmly up here, and walked out again with my jewelry box while we were out riding."

"Not anyone," Trixie pointed out. "How about Patch?"

"His barking in the daytime," Jim said, "doesn't mean a thing. I've got to start training him soon. He barks at the mailman, the bakery truck, the garbage collectors, anything that appears with four wheels."

"If you don't train him soon," Trixie said with a giggle, "he'll be just another Reddy. He's hopeless." She scrambled to her feet. "If anyone has your box, Honey, it's Dick. And it won't take him long to find the secret compartment. What'll he do when he realizes that he went to all that trouble for an antique jewelry box and some costume jewelry?"

"I don't know," Honey said with a sigh. "I've just about decided to become a dress designer instead of a detective. What will he do, Jim?"

"What will who do?" Jim asked.

"Who do, voodoo," Mart said, waving his hands. "Mumbo-jumbo. Now you see it, and now you don't. What he'll do, of course, is sneak the box back into the house the first chance he gets. *If* it was Dick who swiped it," he added. "He certainly can't risk keeping a feminine object like that in his room over the garage for very long. If a tramp swiped it, he'll hack it to pieces and leave the wreckage in the woods."

"I keep telling you," Trixie said crossly, "that a tramp couldn't have swiped it. He might have been hiding in the thicket and heard Honey tell me that she put the diamond in her jewelry box, but he still had no way of knowing which room was Honey's. Even with a floor plan, it would have taken him too long to open all the doors on this floor and peek into every room. Someone downstairs would have heard him."

"That's true," Brian said thoughtfully. "The finger of suspicion does begin to point toward Dick."

"Begin to?" Trixie sniffed. "It has always pointed to

him. If the jewelry box suddenly shows up again, will you believe me?"

"I'll have to," Jim said reluctantly. "Nobody else except Nailor would dare risk being caught on this floor. And Nailor is above suspicion."

"Are you sure of that, Jim?" Brian asked. "What I mean is, maybe Nailor isn't Nailor, but someone else masquerading as him."

Mart howled with laughter. "No matter how you tried you couldn't turn yourself into a giant peanut. Only age and too much work in the hot sun can do that."

"Come on, let's go swimming," Trixie said. "We'll be in late for lunch, anyway; but maybe we can jump in and out of the cold water and dress quickly enough so we won't get a bawling out."

"You girls go ahead," Jim said. "We haven't time. We'll just wash up a bit."

Honey and Trixie raced down to the boathouse, dove into the lake, and climbed right back up again. Then they hurried into the house to change.

"I hope your mother doesn't mind our dripping all over her carpets," Trixie said.

Honey giggled. "We're not dripping. It's so hot, I'm almost dry already. And hotter than ever from hurrying." She started into Jim's old room, then stopped, pointing.

"Oh, Trixie, *look!* There it is on the bureau. My jewelry box. You were right. It was Dick!"

Trixie stared. "Nothing makes sense any more," she moaned. "If Dick swiped it while we were out riding, he couldn't possibly have had time to examine it thoroughly and put it back in the house. He's been as busy as anything ever since he arrived this morning." They quickly changed into the coolest playsuits they could find and dashed downstairs just as Miss Trask was going into the dining-room.

"My, you girls look hot!" she said, smiling. "I really think you look hotter than you feel. It was simply broiling in the village this morning. Are you sure you all want to go to the movies this evening?"

"Oh, yes," Honey said. "The Cameo is air-conditioned."

"In that case," Miss Trask said emphatically, "I'll go with you. We'll all pile into the station wagon. Dick has done a lot of driving today, and the heat hasn't helped his poison ivy rash any. It would do him good to stay quietly in the suite over the garage and watch the wrestling matches with Regan."

Jim sighed. "I guess I won't get a driving lesson. Not until the heat wave breaks."

"Oh, no," Miss Trask said as she served the ice-cold

shrimp salad. "Dick doesn't want to postpone that, Jim. I tried to persuade him to let it go for another day, but he said he'd be all ready for you in the Ford around five. That reminds me," she went on, turning to Honey. "We should go to the early show. Otherwise, you children won't be in bed until midnight. That means we'd better have a light supper at six-thirty, so we can leave at seven-fifteen."

"It would be nice if we could," Honey said. "Will Celia and the cook object?"

"Oh, I don't think so," Miss Trask said. "They're both worn out. This hot, humid weather is exhausting. I'm sure they'd be delighted to retire to their air-conditioned rooms on the third floor."

"I'd like to retire there right now," Mart said with a chuckle. "How come the third floor has air-conditioning, but the rest of the house hasn't? Not that it's any of my business."

Miss Trask smiled at him. "Another simple explanation, Mart. The nearer the roof you get, the hotter it is. The whole house is insulated, of course, but we found that during July and August the rooms on the third floor were too hot for comfort. So Mr. Wheeler had them air-conditioned."

"I think I'll resign as farmer," Mart said, grinning,

"and take on the job of chef. Home was never like the cook's quarters here."

Miss Trask looked puzzled, and Honey quickly explained about the clubhouse and how they all wanted to earn the money so they could make the necessary repairs.

"This," Miss Trask said, "is the nicest thing that ever happened to me. If you boys take over the lawns and the vegetable garden, I know Nailor will never leave us." She sighed. "He complained so much about the heat this morning while he was mowing that I had to give him the rest of the weekend off. He left with Helen and won't be back until Monday morning although his work isn't half-finished." She turned to Honey. "And as for you, my dear, isn't it wonderful that you're going to have a chance to earn some money? I know how you've envied Trixie her job."

Honey smiled happily. "I've been green with envy ever since I've known her. And to think, Miss Trask, I'm to get fifty cents an hour from Mr. Belden just for mending. Why, if there's enough to do, I could make five dollars a week, too!"

"Don't worry about the amount," Trixie said, giggling. "There's always a huge basketful at our house. Bobby never ties his shoelaces, so there are never any heels in his socks. You all know about his shoulder straps, and you've seen the knee-patches on the jeans Brian, Mart, and I wear."

"Next to darning," Honey said dreamily, "I love patching the best."

"It's nice," Brian said to Miss Trask, "to know a girl who likes to do girlish things. Our sister must have been frightened by a darning needle in the cradle."

Celia came in then to clear the table for dessert. Trixie glared at Brian. "Says you! I love darning needles when they're dragonflies. My first pet was one, and after that I collected walking sticks. They're the cutest bugs ever, except for the praying mantis."

"I hate bugs," Honey said. "No, I don't mean that. I'm just a sissy. I'm scared of them. I'm even scared of Bobby's leopard frogs, although they *are* pretty."

"Most girls," Mart said, "*are* afraid of bugs. It's the normal thing to expect, and more fun. Trix is no fun at all. I tried to scare her with a garter snake when she was Bobby's age, but she made a pet out of it and sicked it on me."

"That's not true," Trixie stormed. "It was a great big, black snake. And I never sicked it on you. You teased it until it finally chased you into the pond."

Celia, by this time, was laughing so hard she had to

set her tray down on the table for a minute. "Honest-to-goodness, Miss Trask," she said, "these Beldens will be the death of me. That Bobby! When he helped Jim and Honey move, he got everything mixed up. When I dusted Jim's room this morning, I found Honey's dainty little jewelry box on her dressing table. It looked so silly sitting there in the middle of Jim's fishing tackle, I took it right across the hall and put it on the bureau in his old room." Still shaking with laughter, she picked up the tray and went through the swinging door into the butler's pantry.

No one said anything for a long minute. It was Mart who finally broke the silence. He cleared his throat and said, "That was the best shrimp salad I ever tasted, Miss Trask. Could we have it again for supper this evening?"

"That's a wonderful idea, Mart," she cried. "Why don't we just have a pot-luck supper this evening and give Celia and the cook the whole afternoon off? We can raid the icebox and finish up the leftovers."

"I love leftovers," Honey cried. "No matter what it is, I always think it tastes better the next day, but our cooks almost never let us have delicious things like the Beldens do. They have warmed-up stews and fried macaroni-and-cheese and chocolate bread puddings."

Celia appeared then with strawberry sherbet in strawberry-shaped crystal dishes.

Mart glared at Honey. "Don't mention bread pudding in the presence of that divine-looking ambrosia." He kicked Trixie under the table. "Our frail, feminine sister is especially fond of strawberries. In any shape or form, she adores them. Even when they're stuffed with rocks, she finds them delicious."

Celia giggled. "You mean seeds, Mart, not rocks."

"In Alaska," Mart told her, "which is the land of the midnight sun, practically, strawberries grow to giant size. The seeds must grow, too."

"Oh, stop it, Mart," Trixie said, kicking *him* under the table. "We'll all catch pneumonia if we even think about Alaska in this weather."

"If you had my superior education," Mart said, "you would know that Alaska is the hottest place in the world, practically, during its short summer. Why, the mosquitoes get so big they steal children Bobby's age right off the doorsteps." He turned to Brian. "Next time I'm a junior counselor I must remember to import mosquitoes from Alaska."

"You'll never get another chance at a job like that," Trixie informed him briskly, "not unless you stop exaggerating. I studied about Alaska in school, too, Mart; and the mosquitoes do not grow *quite* to the size of eagles."

Miss Trask laughed. "But they *are* a problem. One has to wear special head-nets and gloves for protection against Alaskan mosquitoes." She turned to Celia. "We've decided to raid the icebox this evening, so you and Cook won't have to fix our supper. Why don't you fill the gallon Thermos jug with iced tea and make a big platter of sandwiches for Regan and Dick? Then they can eat whenever they want to."

"Thank you very much, Miss Trask," Celia said gratefully. "It's so hot! Cook and I were just saying we'd like nothing better than to spend the afternoon and evening in our cool sitting room listening to the radio."

"Then do just that, by all means," Miss Trask said. "I'm going to take the children to the early show at the Cameo. When you see Dick, you might tell him that, except for Jim's driving lesson, he can spend the rest of the day trying to keep cool, too."

"He'll like that," Celia said. "It's not my place to say this, Miss Trask, but Dick is not like Regan. Not *at all* like Regan."

"Were you the one who sent him to us, Celia?" Honey asked suddenly. "Remember? On Wednesday you said you'd ask around in the village and try to find someone who wanted a job as a chauffeur."

Celia patted her dainty ruffled cap. "I did ask around all that afternoon. I asked everyone. And I found just the man for you; but when I came back to work, I found that Dick had already got the job." She disappeared through the swinging door.

Mart winked at Brian. "I can guess who, or should I say whom, Celia had in mind, can't you?"

Brian chuckled. "Tom Delanoy, of course."

"Oh, for Pete's sake," Trixie groaned. "I should have thought of him myself."

"And who," Miss Trask said, "is Tom Delanoy?"

"Regan's twin," Mart said promptly. "Except that he's got black hair and blue eyes. And he likes both cars *and* horses, not to mention kids of all ages. He's a natural for the chauffeuring job here, Miss Trask. He'll shovel the driveway and the paths in the winter and help with the transplanting in the spring. He's handy with a paint brush, too. There isn't anything Tom can't or won't do."

"My goodness," Miss Trask cried. "He sounds perfect, or should I say super? How does one interview him? I have a feeling Dick isn't going to like it here when the snow flies."

"Tom," Brian told her, "taught Mart and me how to shoot and fish. He's about Regan's age and has had all kinds of jobs. He's ready to settle down now; I think he'd like the chauffeur's job here."

"If I were you," Mart said to Miss Trask, "I'd interview Tom right away. *I* have a feeling Dick isn't going to like it here after the first *leaves* fall."

Miss Trask wrung her hands nervously. "But where is Tom now, Mart? How can I get in touch with him?"

"That I don't know," Mart admitted. "Have you any idea what Tom is doing at the moment, Trix?"

Trixie sighed. "It's all too, too uncanny. He's collecting tickets at the Cameo. Miss Trask can talk to him this evening."

"Oh, *that* Tom," Jim cried. "He's a swell guy, Miss Trask. I've run into him in the village often, and we've had long talks. He was the one who recommended the book on pointers I sent away for. I never knew his last name. Never asked him what it was."

"He *is* nice," Honey said. "I don't know him as well as you do, Jim; but one afternoon when I went in to the movies by myself in a taxi, I found I'd forgotten to bring any money. Tom lent me some so I could pay the cab and buy a ticket."

"I remember that time," Miss Trask said, smiling. "I hope *you* remembered to pay him back, Honey."

"Oh, I did," Honey said as they all trooped out to the

porch. "Please talk to him tonight, Miss Trask. If he likes cars and horses, he can't like his job at the Cameo. And Dick—well, he's all right, I guess—but he *is* rude to Trixie."

Miss Trask's crisp gray eyebrows shot up with surprise. "Rude to Trixie? Honey, why didn't you tell me that before?"

"It doesn't matter at all, Miss Trask," Trixie said hastily. "I made fun of him, first. I didn't realize he was just kidding me when he said Jupe kicked him."

Miss Trask sank down in a wicker rocking chair. "What are you talking about? When was Jupiter supposed to have kicked Dick?"

"The black eye," Trixie explained. "That's how he got it. At least, that's what Dick told me."

Miss Trask frowned thoughtfully. "That isn't what he told me. He said he woke in the night when it was pitch black and, not being used to his new room, stumbled, and banged his head against the door which leads into the sitting room. I thought *you* must have awakened him, Trixie, when you screamed during your nightmare."

Trixie grinned. "I probably did, so that makes us all even. He was rude to me, but, indirectly, I gave him a black eye."

Miss Trask's blue eyes twinkled. "But he mustn't be rude to you, Trixie. I'll speak to him about it."

She rocked back and forth. "I'm quite sure Dick was speaking the truth when he said he stumbled and fell Thursday night. You know, Trixie, that the windows of my room face the garage. After we'd gone back to bed and while the old clock was still striking midnight, I heard thumps and bangs. At the time, I thought they had been made by Patch on the porch. He is as restless as we are on hot nights. But when Dick told me how he got his black eye, I realized that it must have been he, falling in the darkness."

Trixie said nothing, but she thought she knew the answer to the thumps and bangs Miss Trask had heard on Thursday night. Dick *had* been in a fight that night—a fight with the man he had tried to double-cross.

Mr. Leather Heels, seeking revenge, had probably been following his trail ever since he regained consciousness after the Tuesday night quarrel. By asking at various dogwagons along the river, he could have traced the green jalopy in a circle that ended at the second set of footprints and tire treadmarks on the shoulder of Glen Road.

It was Mr. Leather Heels, Trixie decided, who had

trampled away the clues. He might have been hiding in the cottage on Thursday and had seen Dick, in his chauffeur's uniform, driving the Wheelers' cars. Between then and midnight, Mr. Leather Heels had merely bided his time. When Dick sneaked back into the garage after trying to steal Honey's jewelry box, he had walked right into the arms of the man he had tried to double-cross.

"Dick," Trixie said to Honey later while the boys were making Bobby's scooter, "didn't stumble into a door Thursday night. According to Mart, that's what everyone says to explain how he got a black eye."

"Well, how did he get it then?" Honey demanded.

Trixie grinned. "According to *Brian,* when a boy comes home with a black eye he got in a fight he tells his father, 'You ought to see the other fellow.' "

Honey gasped. "Mr. Leather Heels! Someone trampled up the clues in the cottage and near the road. It must have been he. He came back and had a fight with Dick!"

"That's what *I* think," Trixie said. "Regan was away, and Patch was shut up on the porch. If the two men had a fight, it would explain a lot of things."

Honey nodded. "The black eye and the noises Miss Trask heard. What else?"

"It would also explain," Trixie said, "why Dick left on Friday and didn't come back until this morning. My guess is that he spent that time trying to find the man who blacked his eye. Because I think that same man knocked Dick out Thursday night and took all of the loot, except, of course, the diamond, away from him."

"The suitcase," Honey interrupted. "The loot was in Dick's suitcase. Remember? You said he was very rude when Regan offered to carry it up to the top of the garage for him."

"That's right," Trixie said. "But I don't think it's there anymore. I think Mr. Leather Heels has it, and that's why Dick must be bound and determined now to get the diamond for his share." She leaned forward to whisper. "I'm sure he'll walk into our trap tonight, Honey. I'm sure of it."

Chapter 17
Where Is Jim?

At five o'clock Jim left with Dick in the Ford for a steering lesson. Honey and Trixie kept as cool as they could down by the lake. Brian was mowing a lawn, and Mart was working in the vegetable garden.

"I should be mending," Honey said. "Your brothers make me feel guilty."

"Pooh," Trixie said with a sniff. "They had a long, lovely vacation at camp. You know perfectly well kids Bobby's age aren't nearly as much trouble as they try to make out."

Honey climbed up the ladder to the boathouse porch and pulled off her cap. "As soon as we dry off a bit," she said, "we ought to get dressed, so we can help Miss Trask take things out of the refrigerator and fix the leftovers attractively."

"Okay," Trixie said. "I hope there's some sherbet left. It's the only thing I feel like eating. I stuffed at lunch."

"I don't think anybody will be very hungry," Honey said. "It's so horribly hot. But let's go and help Miss

Trask. It was darling of her to offer to take us to the movies."

"She's always darling about everything," Trixie agreed. She looked at the clock inside the boathouse and whistled. "It's almost six-thirty. We'll have to hurry."

They trudged up the path, and just then the Ford appeared on the driveway. Dick was at the wheel, but there was no sign of Jim.

"Now, where could he have gone?" Trixie asked crossly. "If he stopped off somewhere, we'll be late to the movies."

They hurried across the driveway to where Dick was parking the Ford. "Where's Jim?" Honey asked.

Dick got out of the car and said, "I took him into the village after his lesson. Said he wanted to get a crew cut like Mart's. He roasted while he was mowing the lawn earlier."

"But where is he now?" Honey asked worriedly. "We're going to have supper soon and go to the movies."

Dick shrugged. "He said not to wait supper for him. He's going to have a bite at the dogwagon and meet you at the Cameo."

"Oh," Honey said in a relieved tone of voice. "I thought he might be planning to walk home after his haircut. He'd never get here in time for supper if he did."

Trixie was staring at Dick. "Did you say Jim was going to eat in the dogwagon?" she asked in a puzzled tone of voice. "Why, he hates that place."

Dick walked away without bothering to reply, and Honey bit her lip. They hurried into the house, and while they changed into cool, cotton dresses, she said, "It makes me furious. Dick is *so* rude to you, Trixie."

"Skip it," Trixie said cheerfully. "Let's put our bait back in its proper place. We'll catch him in our trap at midnight, and then it'll be my turn to be rude to him."

Together, they returned the jewelry box to Honey's dressing table in the room across the hall. "Wasn't it a scream," Honey asked when they were back in Jim's former room, "the way neither of us noticed the box on the bureau in here this morning? If it had been a snake, it would have bitten me."

"Me, too," Trixie admitted ruefully. "But after all, Honey, while we were getting ready to go swimming before lunch, we both had our minds on forged signatures."

Miss Trask came in then and sat down on the window seat. "It hardly seems worthwhile taking food out of the refrigerator. Brian and Mart said they couldn't eat a thing, and Jim won't be home. How do you girls feel about food?"

"We're not a bit hungry," Honey said. "Let's have a picnic supper when we get back from the movies. It should be cooler then."

"A good idea," Miss Trask said. She glanced at Honey appraisingly. "Your hair should be trimmed, dear. I don't blame Jim at all for getting a crew cut."

"Is he really going to?" Trixie asked curiously. "Did he tell you that when he phoned, Miss Trask?"

"Why, no," Miss Trask said. "He didn't phone, Trixie. He sent word by Dick that he would meet us in the Cameo lobby at seven-thirty."

"He didn't phone!" Trixie repeated, surprised. "Why, even Mart has better manners than that. I can't believe Jim would make plans without asking your permission, Miss Trask. The line must be out of order."

Miss Trask smiled. "It isn't really a question of manners, Trixie. Jim is very independent, you know. And he's so sensible. I never worry about him."

"I still think the line must be out of order," Trixie said stubbornly. "It wasn't like Jim not to call you."

Miss Trask sighed. "Both the phones are working, dear. I'm so hot I telephoned Regan instead of walking across to the garage. I just called him a minute ago to tell him that we're going to leave all the doors and windows open. We don't want to shut in the hot air and shut out the cool air, but it may rain before we get back."

"I hope it pours," Honey said and added quickly, "Oh, no, I don't. If it does, Regan will have to leave the television set while he and Dick close the house. Regan is wild about the wrestling matches."

"I know," Miss Trask said with another sigh. "But Celia and the cook are just as wild about the Saturday evening radio programs. Maybe we should shut up the house ourselves and leave them all in peace."

"Oh, let's not," Honey pleaded. "I'd rather come back and find every room a swimming pool than shut out an inch of cool evening air."

Miss Trask glanced out of the window at the gray-blue sky. "I have it," she said suddenly. "I like to watch the wrestling matches, too, although I'm not quite as wild about them as Regan is. I'll drop you children off at the movies, and then I'll invite myself to share Mr. Lytell's television set with him. He's asked me to a dozen times, and his home is so near I could get back here in plenty of time to prevent swimming pools at the first drop of rain."

Honey threw her arms around Miss Trask. "Everyone leaves the worst chores to you," she cried. "It's not fair. You go to the movies with Trixie and the boys. I'll stay here and keep an eye on things."

"I'll stay with you," Trixie said quickly. She grinned at Miss Trask. "You don't really want to miss two hours in an air-cooled theater, do you?"

Miss Trask chuckled. "You're both sweet, generous girls; but I honestly do like television at times. And Mr. Lytell is a rather lonely old man. I'll have a pleasant evening with him and pick you children up in front of the Cameo at nine-thirty."

"You'll have a pleasant evening *if* it doesn't rain," Honey pointed out. "Besides, the wrestling matches don't start until nine."

"Oh, there are other programs," Miss Trask said cheerfully. "No, my mind's made up. I'll go and telephone Mr. Lytell right now and prepare him for my company."

"I know," Honey cried. "Why can't we come home in a taxi, Miss Trask? Then you can stay right on at Mr. Lytell's and see all the wrestling matches."

"That's it," Trixie said. "We can all chip in and pay for the cab now that we're wage earners."

"That's right," Honey said, smiling. "I'll have to borrow fifteen cents from you, Trixie, until I darn the first batch of socks. Please say yes, Miss Trask. You haven't had any time off in ages."

"We-ell," Miss Trask said doubtfully.

"You couldn't possibly worry about us for a minute," Trixie said. "You just said yourself that Jim is super-sensible. And Celia and the cook will still be awake when we get back. So will Regan."

Miss Trask chuckled again. "As Mart would say, 'You twisted my arm.' All right. I'll probably be back home while you're still raiding the refrigerator." She frowned. "I was looking forward to meeting your friend, Tom Delanoy, Trixie; but I suppose that can wait."

"Of course, it can," Honey said, giving her an affectionate pat. "We'll interview him for you. I need practice anyway if I'm going to be Mother's private secretary for a birthday present."

"That's a very good idea, Honey," Miss Trask said approvingly. "Although you're only thirteen, you *are* the young lady of the house. If you do a good job of interviewing Dick's successor, I'll have other tasks for you. What are you going to say to him?"

"I'm going to tell him the truth," Honey said promptly. "You know perfectly well, Miss Trask, that you made up your mind to fire Dick on September first, as soon as you heard he was rude to Trixie."

"What a mind reader you are," Miss Trask said with a broad grin. "I instantly decided he could keep the advance salary we gave him in lieu of two weeks' notice.

I'd rather do all the driving myself than have a rude employee on the place."

Honey giggled. "And as soon as I heard about Tom Delanoy, I made up my mind that you'd want him to start work right after Labor Day."

"Good for you," Miss Trask said. "With the help of Trixie and her brothers, maybe you can persuade him to do just that."

"And Jim," Trixie added. "Don't forget that Tom is a good friend of Jim's, too."

Miss Trask nodded. "We've certainly settled a lot of things in such a short time. I guess your brothers have had a swim and changed by now, Trixie. I'll go call Mr. Lytell and then get the station wagon out of the garage."

Half an hour later, she let them out in front of the Cameo Theater. "Be good, boys and girls," she said, waving from behind the wheel. "And have fun."

Trixie hastily pushed her way through the crowded lobby to the ticket collector's stand. "Hi, Tom," she said. "Has Jim gone in yet? Jim Frayne, you know. The redheaded boy our neighbors adopted last month."

"No, he hasn't," Tom Delanoy said. "I haven't seen him since we both had haircuts in the barber shop last week."

Trixie blinked. "Did Jim have a haircut just last week?"

The tall, good-looking young man stared at her. "What's so remarkable about that? You need a haircut yourself, and so does Honey Wheeler."

Honey, who had followed closely behind Trixie, giggled. "If this weather keeps up, I think I'll get a crew cut like Mart's. Jim was supposed to meet us here at seven-thirty, Tom. Sure he didn't go in ahead of us?"

"Not unless he was wearing a wig," Tom said. "Which I very much doubt in this heat. If you kids are smart, you'll go in and hold a seat for Jim. The place is filling up fast."

"We'd better do that," Brian said, producing the four tickets he had just bought. "Jim probably got delayed getting a bite in the dogwagon. It's always packed and jammed on Saturdays at this time."

They all filed inside and soon discovered that the Cameo was packed and jammed too. Trixie and Honey finally found two seats together on the aisle.

"I don't know where the boys went to," Trixie whispered. "And I couldn't care less. I'm so worried about Jim I can't stand it."

"But why?" Honey whispered back.

"Sh-h," Trixie cautioned her. "We'll be asked to

leave." She sat rigidly in her seat and tried to concentrate on the newsreel, but she could think of nothing but Jim.

Jim hadn't telephoned Miss Trask to get permission to have a crew cut and supper in the village.

Jim had just had a haircut last week.

Jim didn't like to eat in the dogwagon. Jim liked to raid the icebox.

Jim had said he would be waiting for them in the lobby at seven-thirty. Jim was prompt. And they had been late, because Miss Trask had had to stop for gas on the way in.

When last seen, Jim had gone off for a driving lesson with Dick. Dick. Dick.

On a lonely country road. A lonely country road. A lonely country road.

It became a maddening little tune that shut out all other sounds. "Dick and a lonely country road. Dick and a lonely country road."

Then Trixie remembered something else that made her sit up even straighter. Bobby had probably told Dick that Honey and Jim had switched rooms. And he must have told him, too, that the "boxlike thing" had not been switched.

Dick would know that he could not hope to sneak into the house at night and steal the jewelry box if Jim was sleeping in Honey's old room. Therefore, Dick somehow had to get rid of Jim. That was why he had offered to give Jim driving lessons—on a lonely country road. That was why Dick had planned his whole day so that nothing would interfere with the driving lesson.

Trixie shivered. She nudged Honey's arm. "Come out to the rest room with me," she whispered. "I'm so worried about Jim I can't stand it."

There was no one else in the little powder room when the girls got there. Honey's hazel eyes widened when Trixie told her what she had been thinking all during the movie.

"But, Trixie," she gasped. "You forget one thing. Dick knew that we were all going to the early show and wouldn't be back until after nine-thirty. He also knew that Celia and the cook would have their ears glued to the radio all evening and that Regan would be glued to the television set once the wrestling matches started. Between nine and nine-thirty this evening would be a perfect time for Dick to go in and get my jewelry box. He didn't have any reason to get rid of Jim during that time, because he knew Jim was going to the movies, too."

Trixie jumped. "Oh, my goodness, I never thought of that!" She leaned over to look at the watch on Honey's wrist. "The wrestling matches don't start for another half-hour. Dick wouldn't dare try to sneak out of the garage and into the house before then. Regan might hear him." She sighed disappointedly. "You've got to call Regan right away, Honey, and tell him everything. We'll have to let him catch Dick in our trap."

But Honey wasn't listening. "I think I know where Jim is," she said slowly. "He's so smart, he must have figured out long ago that Dick would try to get the diamond out of my jewelry box while we were at the movies. Don't you see, Trixie? Jim got Dick to leave him off in the village after the driving lesson, and then he walked home. He's probably hiding in the closet of my old room right now."

"But Jim doesn't suspect Dick," Trixie cried impatiently.

"I think he does now," Honey said. "I didn't want to tell you before, because I thought you might be cross with Mart. But while you were telephoning your father before lunch, Mart looked at the crumpled sheets of paper we threw into Jim's scrap basket. He knew right off that we'd been trying to prove how easily Dick could have forged Mr. Whitney's signature. Jim was very impressed when he saw how the M and W in my name were slightly blurred. I have a feeling that he decided, then and there, to look at that reference. If he did, and found traces of carbon on the signature—"

"Honey," Trixie interrupted. "That must be just what happened. While we were having a swim before lunch, Jim must have found out that Mr. Whitney's signature looked suspicious. Remember how quiet he was during lunch? The rest of us did a lot of kidding, but he hardly spoke a word."

Honey nodded. "I think he was planning, then, to catch Dick in our trap. That's why he didn't come home after the driving lesson. Jim wanted to make sure that Dick knew that he was out of the way."

Trixie shook her head. "That wasn't exactly necessary. I mean, Jim getting Dick to leave him off in the village. If Jim had left for the movies with us in the station wagon, Dick would have seen him and would have thought that Jim would be out of the way between nine and nine-thirty. Jim could have gone inside the Cameo with the rest of us, and then gone right out again. There still would have been time for him to have walked home and hidden in your closet." Nervously, she unknotted her handkerchief in which she had put some change, the girls' share of the taxi on the return trip. "Here's a nickel," she told Honey. "Call your house. If Jim's there, I won't worry about anything. Hurry. It's a quarter to nine."

Honey hurried to the booth and dialed her number. Then she stood there, waiting.

It seemed like hours to Trixie, and she couldn't stand it. "No answer?" she asked. "What's the matter?"

Honey put the receiver back on the hook. "The line's out of order, Trixie. It must be thundering and lightning like anything."

"I don't believe it," Trixie cried impatiently. "A bad electric storm couldn't have come up so quickly. You probably dialed the wrong number."

Honey meekly took the nickel out of the returned-coins box and put it back in the slot. This time, she dialed the operator. "I'm trying to get Sleepyside six-oh-three-oh-three," she said. "Could you tell me, please, if the line is out of order?"

After a minute the operator said something Trixie couldn't hear, and the nickel jangled in the box. "It *is* out of order," Honey told Trixie. "Electric storms do come up quickly along the river." She slipped her slim fingers in for the nickel and started out of the booth.

Trixie pushed her back inside. "Try Regan's number. Both lines can't be down. They just can't be."

Honey sighed, but she dropped the nickel in the slot for the third time and dialed another number. In a few seconds Trixie heard the operator's voice. She had crowded as far into the booth as she could to listen.

"Sor-ree, that line is out of order."

Honey hung up, and the nickel jangled in the box. "Oh, Trixie," she cried, "please don't worry about Jim. Maybe he's right here in the theater sitting with Brian and Mart. They were going to sit near the back and keep an eye out for him. Maybe Jim came in right after we did."

"Maybe he did," Trixie admitted as she led the way out of the rest room. "Let's go ask Tom Delanoy."

Outside, they found Tom sitting on a folding chair which he had placed on the sidewalk in front of the theater. The sidewalk, Trixie noted, was dry. "Did Jim come in?" she asked Tom.

He shook his head. "Nobody's come in since the feature started," he said.

"Has there been much thunder and lightning?"

"Are you kiddin'?" he demanded. "We're not going to get rain. We're not even going to get a breath of cool air. The storm passed right over us."

"It's awfully dark for so early in the evening, with daylight saving and all," Honey said. "Maybe there was an electric storm out in the country where we live."

"Honey Wheeler," he said exasperatedly, "I'm neither blind nor deaf. If there was any turbulence over

Glen Road, I would have known about it. You don't live *that* far out."

Trixie moved closer to him. "Tom," she said, "I've got to go right home. Will you, please, get me a cab and lend me fifty cents?"

He stood up, grinning as he reached into his pocket for two quarters. "Anything for Brian and Mart Belden's kid sister. But what's the hurry, Trixie?"

"I can't explain now," Trixie said. "Oh, there's a cab. Grab it for me, please, Tom."

Tom went to the curb, whistling through his fingers.

"I'm going with you," Honey said, frowning. "I don't understand why both lines are out of order. Remember? Miss Trask called Mr. Lytell just before we left."

"You're *not* coming with me," Trixie said determinedly. "You stay right here and interview Tom about the job. When I get to your house, I'll probably find that everything's all right. There's no sense in both of us going."

"But suppose you don't find that everything's all right," Honey said nervously. "Suppose you—"

"Never mind," Trixie interrupted. "There'll be an intermission soon, and a lot of people will leave. Brian and Mart will come out here looking for us, so we can all sit together for the second feature. You'll have to be here, so you can explain why I left."

"We-ell," Honey said dubiously, "I guess you're right, Trixie, but I'd rather go with you. Not that I'd be much help if you did run into trouble."

The taxi, on the other side of the intersection, had come to a halt when Tom Delanoy whistled, but as the driver turned and headed toward the Cameo, the traffic light changed to red.

"Just my luck," Trixie moaned as she and Honey joined Tom at the curb. "It never fails. Whenever you're in a hurry the light's always against you."

"What *is* your hurry anyway?" Tom demanded suspiciously. "You're in some sort of a scrape, Trixie Belden. I can tell."

Trixie ignored him and nudged Honey. "Well, go ahead," she said. "This is as good a time as any for you to interview Tom."

"Interview *me?*" Tom's eyebrows shot up in surprise. "What am I, a celebrity or something?" He tipped his cap and bowed deeply. "Perhaps," he said, mincing his words, "you would like my autograph, ladies?"

Honey giggled, rather nervously, Trixie thought. "Not that kind of interview, Tom. We're going to need a new chauffeur pretty soon. Brian and Mart told us that you would be perfect—just the kind of chauffeur we need. You'll like Regan, too. He's our groom. You'll share his apartment above our garage. It's really very nice, with a radio and a television set and all." She stopped, her pretty face flushed with embarrassment. "Oh, Tom, what I'm trying to say is, will you accept? *Please* do!"

"Wow!" Tom's eyes sparkled. "Gee, Honey, that job sounds like the answer to my prayers. Just say the word. When do I start?"

"Right after Labor Day, if you can." Honey let out a long sigh of relief. "I never thought interviewing would be that easy. I think I'm going to enjoy being Mother's secretary."

The light had at last changed and the cab was drawing up to the curb in front of the theater. Tom opened the door and Trixie hastily clambered inside.

"Crabapple Farm," Tom said to the driver. "The Belden place on Glen Road." He slammed the door and touching the vizor of his cap as though he were already a chauffeur, grinned at Trixie.

She waved to him and Honey and settled tensely back on the cushion. It seemed like hours before the cab had threaded its way through the crowded section of the village. Then Trixie leaned forward.

"I've changed my mind," she said to the driver. "I want to go to the Manor House. It's the next driveway after ours. You can just leave me off at the mailbox. The Wheelers' mailbox you know."

"I know it well," the taxi driver said, stepping on the gas as they left the town behind. "And I'm glad you don't want me to take you up that hill. The last time I tried to make the turn by the garage I clipped the heads off a few hollyhocks." He chatted on and on, predicting an isolated life for the Wheelers when winter set in and the steep driveway would be a sheet of ice.

But Trixie didn't listen. She sat tensely on the back seat, thinking.

Someone deliberately cut the telephone wires so that he wouldn't be disturbed. Even with their ears glued to the radio, Celia and the cook would know if the phone rang and rang, for there was an extension bell in the servants' sitting room on the third floor. No matter how noisy the wrestling matches might be, Regan would hear the phone in the suite over the garage, because it was on a table right by the television set.

Someone had carefully cut the wires in case someone should telephone to find out why Jim hadn't appeared at the Cameo.

Therefore, something had happened to Jim!

Trixie closed her eyes. Dick and Jim on that lonely road! Jim, who had previously examined the signature on Dick's letter of recommendation and found traces of carbon. Jim, with his redheaded hot temper. Jim was probably thinking, "This fellow tried to make fools of all of us. He took advantage of little Bobby's trusting nature. He was mean and nasty to Trixie who rightly suspected him all along. I've a good mind to black his other eye for him."

Trixie moaned inwardly. Jim was so honest it would have been hard for him to disguise the fact that he suspected Dick of forgery, if not of robbery. Try as he probably did, he must have said something, or let Dick know by the expression on his freckled face, that he had an idea who the midnight prowler was. And then—and then—

"Here we are," the taxi driver said. "Seventy-five cents. Sure you can make your way up that hill in the dark?"

Trixie gave him the money and hopped out. "I know it better than I do my own face," she said. "I practically live here." She slammed the door and started off at a run. Halfway up the driveway, she stopped. Both the radio on the third floor of the house and the television set in the garage were blaring. From where she stood, it looked as though not a single light was burning on the first or second floors.

Someone with a tiny flashlight was climbing stealthily up the side steps to the screen door of the wide veranda.

Trixie left the graveled driveway and hurried along the lawn, tensely listening. Would Patch bark, or would he fawn on the person who was now entering the house?

Chapter 18
A Dim Light

Patch did not bark; and by the time Trixie groped her way up the front steps of the veranda, there was no sign of the man with the dim flashlight. It was pitch black on the porch; and Trixie jumped when Patch's cold, moist nose touched her hand.

She hesitated. Suppose the person with the flashlight was Jim, getting ready to catch someone in their trap? If she made any noise, she would frighten away the prowler.

Honey's explanation of why Jim hadn't gone to the movies might be the right one. Jim might have walked back, after Dick left him in the village. He might have been hiding in the shrubbery, watching the garage ever since then. He might even now be trailing Dick to Honey's old room, so he could catch him red-handed.

"This I must see," Trixie said to herself as she tip-toed across the porch and into the hall. A dim light was burning at the far end of it, and as soon as her eyes grew accustomed to the semidarkness, she groped her way up the carpeted stairs.

The second-floor hall was dimly lighted by forty-watt bulbs in the ceiling at both ends of it, and Trixie saw at once that the door to Honey's former room was closed.

She moved swiftly down toward it, and, as silently as possible, turned the knob. It made the same faint grating sound which had awakened her on Thursday night; and when she had opened it a crack, Trixie stopped, holding her breath.

Then she peered inside. Someone, who had taped his flashlight so that it gave off only a tiny pencil of light, was examining Honey's jewelry box. Someone with blond, not red, hair, someone who, from the back, looked like Dick.

Trixie stared, not quite knowing what to do. The trap was sprung. They had caught the prowler, and probably the man who had stolen the diamond—but how could she hope to keep him a prisoner?

If she screamed at the top of her lungs, Regan could not possibly hear her above the noisy roar of the wrestling matches, and even if Celia on the floor above did hear her, what could the maid and the cook do?

With the telephone out of order, she couldn't call for help from the police. She couldn't do a thing but stand there, worrying about what might have happened to Jim and wondering if there wasn't some way—

Then, although she was not touching it, the door opened wider and something brushed against Trixie's bare leg. She stifled a scream as Patch bounded across the room to leap up with joyous little whines on the man by the dressing table. He turned, pointing the pencil of light toward the entrance and recognized her at the same moment that she recognized him.

"So," he snarled, "the nosy little girl next door. What brought you home from the movies so soon?"

"You," Trixie said, hoping her voice didn't sound as scared as she felt. "You, Dick. I thought you might pick this time to sneak into the house and try to get the diamond back. Stole it, didn't you?"

He crossed the room in swift strides and grabbed her wrist, dragging her across the threshold and closing the door.

"Bite him, Patch," Trixie said without much hope. "Bite his hand right off."

The black and white puppy looked up at them both adoringly, thumping his tail on the floor.

Dick laughed. "He won't bite me. I had sense enough to make friends with him and your stupid setter from the very beginning."

"Reddy is not stupid," Trixie said staunchly. "Where is Jim?"

He laughed again. "During our little ride this afternoon, I was forced to knock him out and tie him up and gag him. If you must know, he's lying in the woods far enough from that deserted lane so that no one will see him."

Trixie gasped. "You—you, horrible little weasel," she said hotly. "How did you ever dare to do such a thing? Just wait and see what will happen to you."

"Nothing's going to happen to me," he said with an evil chuckle. "After you've given me the diamond, I'm going to tie you up, too. By the time your friends and that bossy governess get back, I'll be miles away." He pointed the pencil of light toward the jewelry box. "Get going, little girl, I haven't much time. Get the rock out of the secret compartment."

It was Trixie's turn to laugh. "It isn't there. It's someplace where you'll never find it."

He gripped her wrist so tightly that Trixie had to clench her teeth to keep from crying out. Lightning forked the sky then, and she could see his face clearly for a moment. He looked so angry that she almost wished she could give him the diamond. Thunder rumbled from across the river.

Trixie swallowed her fright. "You haven't much time, Dick," she said in as cold a voice as she could muster. "Miss Trask will be back to close the windows at the first drop of rain. She's only a five-minute ride away. At Mr. Lytell's."

"Don't try to be funny," he said harshly. "She's in town at the Cameo. And I siphoned most of the gas out of the station wagon so she'll get stuck midway between here and Main Street."

"Very bright of you," Trixie said, forcing her taut lips to smile. "Very bright. And I suppose you did something to the gauge, too, so that it wouldn't register. But Miss Trask happens to be smart about cars. She stopped on the way into town and had the tank filled when she saw the gauge wasn't working. She's extra careful about things like that."

"Stop gabbing," he said. "Where is the rock?"

Trixie thought for a minute. If she could keep him here until it started to rain, Miss Trask would be back. But what could Miss Trask do to keep this thin, ugly man from running away? If he had already knocked out Jim, he wouldn't hesitate to strike anyone who interfered with his plans. And the first thing Miss Trask would do when she returned would be to run right upstairs to close the windows in Mrs. Wheeler's lovely room. She would run right into Dick's clutches.

No, she wouldn't, Trixie decided quickly. *Because*

I'll scream the minute I see headlights in the driveway. I'll scream and scream, and then she'll get Regan before she comes into the house.

"The rock," Dick was hissing close to her ear. "Where is it?"

Trixie pursed her lips and tossed her head. "I'll tell you," she said coyly, "if you'll tell me how you got the black eye. The pal you tried to double-cross came back Thursday night and saw you sneaking into the house, didn't he? He hid in your room over the garage, and when you came back, he beat you up."

He shook her arm roughly. "You know too much, Miss Nosy. When I go, I'll take you with me for a nice, long ride. But first, where is the rock?"

Trixie smiled sweetly. "You and your pal had engine trouble down on the road Tuesday night, so you spent the night in the cottage. You and he had a fight, dividing up the loot, huh? You knocked him out, fixed the motor, and drove away. When you discovered the diamond was missing, you came back. That's when you listened in the thicket and heard Honey tell me where she had put the diamond."

"That's right," he said. "That's right, smarty. But the point is, where is the rock now?"

"Then," Trixie went on, just as though he hadn't

interrupted, "you lurked around in the woods near the stable and heard everyone talking about how much the Wheelers needed a chauffeur. You drove up to the garage Wednesday evening and applied for the job."

He pointed the pencil of light at her face and stared at her. "You sure do get around, don't you? I've got to hand it to you. I suppose you figured out that when I found I had to have references, I stopped off at the mailbox long enough on my way out to borrow a few letters. Only one of them had a signature worth copying, but it sure worked, the signature on that check made out to Matthew Wheeler, Treas."

Trixie laughed, although her throat was so dry it hurt. "Of course, I figured all that out. Anyone can buy tracing and carbon paper and rent a typewriter. Did you put the letter from Mr. Whitney back in the mailbox Thursday afternoon while Bobby was showing you around the place and telling you which windows on this floor were Honey's?"

"Natch," he said, narrowing his eyes. "Think I want to get mixed up with G-men?"

"You're already mixed up with the FBI," Trixie told him, "if you swiped that diamond in another state. And don't worry, they'll catch you. They probably already have your pal. What's his name, anyway?"

"Louie," he growled, his fingers tightening on her wrist. "What makes you think the coppers have nabbed Louie? What do you know about him?"

"I don't *know* anything," Trixie retorted. "I just guessed that after he beat you up Thursday night he took the rest of the loot out of your suitcase. You did keep it in your suitcase, didn't you? That's why you almost had a fit when Regan offered to carry it up to the top of the garage for you?" He merely nodded, glaring, and she went on, hoping it would start to rain soon. "You used the black eye as an excuse, so you could go off yesterday and try to find Louie." She forced a chuckle from her dry throat. "You never went to see a doctor. You've had more black eyes in your life than you've ever had poison ivy. I thought, at first, that the person who stole the diamond and dropped it in the cottage was a fruit picker. But you never worked in the country. If you had, your skin would be tanned, and you'd have known better than to hide in the midst of poison ivy." Again she chuckled dryly. "You've been working in a big city—"

"That I have," he interrupted with a harsh laugh. "The big city of New York, you two-bit dick. Just for being so fresh, I'm going to—"

"Just what *will* you do?" a voice interrupted from

the doorway. There was a small click and the room was suddenly flooded with light.

Trixie whirled around, blinking in the glare of the bright overhead lights. Jim was coming in the room; and, right behind him, loomed Regan, his finger on the trigger of his hunting rifle.

"Reach for the ceiling, Laughing-Boy," Regan said ominously. "I'm a crack shot, right, Jim?"

Jim didn't bother to answer. He crossed over to the window and stared down at the driveway. From where she was standing by the dressing table, Trixie could see the headlights of a car. A prowl car!

"Here come the police," Jim said to Dick who was holding his hands in the air. "Bracelets are going to look nice on your skinny wrists!"

"Oh, Jim," Trixie cried. "He knocked you out and left you in the bushes. How did you get here?"

Jim smiled briefly. "I'm tough. I didn't stay unconscious long. But it took time to get free of the rope he had tied around my wrists and ankles. It was dark by the time I burst into the Hoyts' farmhouse and asked them if I could use their phone." He shrugged. "By that time, I knew that Dick had forged Mr. Whitney's name to the reference Dad showed me. I finally took the hint, Trixie, and

looked at it again. So, when we were having our so-called steering lesson, I asked Dick the Dip—he *is* a pickpocket, Trixie—if he didn't think Mr. Whitney's thick, curly hair made him look like a lion. Dick heartily agreed with me. That did it. He gave himself away, because, you see, Mr. Whitney is as bald as a billiard ball."

"Jim, Jim," Trixie interrupted. "You shouldn't have gone off with him alone. I—" But a big policeman was striding into the room.

"Why, Dapper Dick," he said, patting the thin, frightened-looking man's pockets. "Every state trooper in the county has been looking for you since Tuesday. We picked up Louie early yesterday morning in the dog-wagon. He has a nice case of poison ivy, too." The officer pulled Dick's hands behind his back and manacled them together. "Figured you were close by, but not this close. Where's the rock, Pretty Boy?"

Dick glared at Trixie. "That fresh little girl has it. Why don't you frisk *her?*"

Trixie giggled nervously. "Honey Wheeler and I found the diamond, Officer. My mother has it now. Mrs. Peter Belden, you know. I'll go right home and get it."

"No hurry about that," the policeman said cheerfully. "If your dad's Pete Belden, he can turn it over to the Sarge in the morning. I guess a banker's house is about as safe as the bank itself." He turned to Regan. "Want to ride back to headquarters with me and prefer charges? Breaking and entering, assault and battery—what else?"

"Well, now," Regan said easily, "I don't know as Mr. Wheeler would want to get mixed up in this. The publicity, you know. If you were looking for the guy anyway, you won't need our testimony to hold him, will you?"

The policeman guffawed. "We've got enough on him and Louie to put 'em behind bars until they're old and gray." He gave Dick a playful poke with his nightstick. "Get going, Pretty Boy. For the next few years you won't have to worry about poison ivy."

After they had gone, Trixie collapsed in the nearest chair. "How did the police happen to arrive at such a nice moment?" she asked Jim. "Both the phones are out of order."

"I know," Jim said. "I know all too well. I called the house and the garage from the Hoyts', and then I guessed that Dick had probably cut the wires. I called the police then—I knew the Bob-Whites of the Glen had better not fool around any longer." He grinned. "Then I dashed through the woods as fast as I could."

Trixie stared at him. "What kept you from dashing right up here and getting caught in our own trap, the way I brightly did?"

Jim chuckled. "I saw a speck of moving light in this room, and I figured Dick was busy with Honey's jewelry box. Regan's a good guy, I thought, he won't want to miss the fun. When I told Regan what had happened to me, he quickly decided it would be more fun if he had a loaded gun."

The cheery groom took a deep breath and let it out again. "It wasn't loaded, Jim, my boy. You know I never leave a bullet in my rifle when I'm not using it. But I figured our pickpocket friend wouldn't know the difference."

"Then he really is Dick the Dip," Trixie gasped. "How did you know, Jim?"

"Because," Jim said, "when I accused him of being one of the two men your brothers said state troopers were looking for all along the river, he started to boast. It was just a wild guess, and I should have kept my mouth shut. But as soon as I realized that he'd been making fools of all of us, except you, Trixie, I lost my temper."

"I still don't understand," Trixie said. "People don't go around carrying diamonds that size in their pockets."

"No," Jim said, "but they wear them when they're set in engagement rings. Maybe I'd better begin at the beginning."

"Wait a minute," Trixie interrupted. "Here comes a taxi. The others are back from the movies. Let's raid the icebox while we catch them up on events. Then you can begin at the beginning, Jim."

"This I must hear," Regan said. "You can watch the wrestling matches almost any evening, but you don't often get a chance to find out what you kids have been up to. Am I invited?"

"You certainly are," Trixie said quickly. "No more secrets from you, Regan. Bro*ther,* as Mart would say, was I ever glad to see you standing in the door with that gun!"

Ten minutes later, they were all gathered around the long kitchen table. Regan had donated to the feast the big platter of sandwiches Celia and the cook had made earlier. Honey poured creamy milk into tall glasses as Trixie told Regan how she and Honey had found the diamond.

When she finished, Regan shook his head. "Say, Trixie," he said, almost sternly, "you got off easy with just a bad fright. And what a lucky break for you that I didn't go to the police station and prefer charges. If I

261

had, the cops would have soon found out that your mother has the diamond but doesn't know it. If I had any sense, I'd give you a good bawling out for keeping it from the police so long!"

"Don't worry about that part of it," Brian said. "We're all in trouble. We can't very well ask Dad to take the diamond to headquarters tomorrow without confessing our sins."

"That's true," Regan said in a relieved tone of voice. "How do your parents stand you kids, anyway? What next?"

"I still don't understand about the Dick the Dip part," Honey complained. "Please begin at the beginning as you promised, Jim."

Then Jim explained. "Dick and Louie," he said, "are sort of super-pickpockets. They make a specialty of robbing big New York office buildings during the hot summer months. Firms are not only understaffed, then, with many employees away on vacation, but they're careless. They leave the doors open to the main corridors and then go into adjoining offices, leaving the reception room empty. Women workers," he went on, "are especially careless, according to Dick. Before he bopped me on the head, he boasted plenty."

"Oh, I hate him," Honey cried fiercely. "I hate him.

I hope he has poison ivy all the time he's in jail."

Jim patted her small hand affectionately. "It didn't hurt, Sis. It was just a stunning blow. You see, he was sitting in the back seat, and I was sitting in front behind the wheel. The idea was that I'd get self-confidence more quickly that way. So I didn't even know what was happening until too late."

Trixie gasped. "Why, that sounds as though he planned to knock you out even before you accused him of being a bow—bow—"

"Bogus is the word," Mart said. "Which you would have known, if you had my superior education."

Trixie ignored him. "Bogus chauffeur."

Jim nodded. "He did plan to get rid of me as soon as Bobby told him that Honey and I had switched rooms. That's why he offered to give me driving lessons just before he left to try and find Louie who had knocked *him* out the night before and departed with the rest of the loot."

"So that's why he was so touchy about his suitcase," Regan said. "All the loot but the diamond was in it?"

"That's right," Jim said. "When Dick came back, after finding no trace of Louie, he decided to get the diamond tonight. He planned to get me out of his hair late in the afternoon and say that he left me in the village for a haircut, and so forth. Then, Celia told him that we were all going to the early show. When he heard that, he wasn't interested in the driving lesson any more, but he had to keep his promise in order to avoid suspicion. I don't think he would have bopped me on the head if I hadn't lost my temper and accused him of forgery."

"Red hair," Trixie said with a grin, "will do it every time. Let's get back to women office workers and how careless they are. Not," she added in a loud aside to Honey, "that they're any more careless than men."

Jim shrugged. "According to Dick they are. He says they are forever leaving jewelry and their handbags in a nice spot where, during the hot weather, they can be snatched by anybody strolling along the corridors. Anyway," he went on, "Dick and Louie made a nice haul during July and August. Most of the stuff they snatched wasn't very valuable, but it all amounted to quite a nice haul just the same. The diamond was a windfall—and the pickpockets' downfall."

Honey nodded. "The lady it belonged to must have been furious. Mother would have hysterics if anything happened to the ring Daddy gave her."

"The lady," Jim said, "according to police, was wild. When I called headquarters from the Hoyts', I told the desk sergeant everything I knew about Dick, and he was wild, too. They had been questioning Louie since yesterday morning as to the whereabouts of Dick and the diamond, but Louie, for some reason known only to the brotherhood of dips, wouldn't tell them a thing."

"How did the police get on the trail of Dick and Louie in the first place?" Mart asked. "Trying to catch a sneak thief in one of those big New York office buildings would be like trying to find a needle in a haystack." He bowed to Trixie. "Pardon the expression. I know how you hate the word needle."

"I don't know," Jim said. "The sergeant didn't go into details over the phone. But I imagine that when the lady who owns the diamond discovered it was missing, she raised a hue and a cry pretty quickly. An elevator boy may have been able to describe two suspicious-looking characters he had noticed loitering in the office building just before that."

"Uh-huh," Regan said. "New York police detectives are as familiar with the faces of all known pickpockets as they are with their own. And Dapper Dick, minus the black eye and poison ivy, would have been easy to spot."

"Why, in spite of that," Trixie added, "our very own Sleepyside policemen recognized him right off." She turned to Jim. "I suppose, after they stole the ring, they took it out of the setting, planning to pawn the stone in some town way upstate?"

"I imagine so," Jim said. "Or it may have been jarred from the setting during the fight in the cottage Tuesday night. You were right about that, Trixie; in fact, you were right about practically everything."

"Sometimes, she is," Mart said sadly. "But let's not get in the habit of believing her. If we did, we'd be sure to end up on Mars."

"Is that the next stop?" Regan asked, pretending to cringe. "Flying saucers will be the thing that starts her off, I'll bet." He poured himself another glass of iced tea. "The thing that makes me happiest is that Dick spent a lot of time with Bobby yesterday morning and never had any idea that the kid had the rock in his pocket all the time."

"That makes me happy, too," Trixie said. "But I'll never be really happy, Regan, until you tell us your secret."

"Well, now," he said, crossing his long legs, "things have changed in the last few hours. I doubt if Miss Trask will buy Susie after all."

"Miss Trask," Trixie yelled. "Was *she* going to buy Susie? Why, she doesn't know a thing about horses!"

Regan shrugged his broad shoulders. "She can learn, can't she? If Jim, here, has picked up the gear-shift business so quickly, I guess I could teach Miss Trask a little something about how to make a horse stop and go."

"Regan," Honey cried. "You're just teasing us. Does Miss Trask really want to have riding lessons?"

"That's what she told me," Regan retorted. "Said if I thought Susie was a good buy, she'd buy her on the installment plan. Said we really ought to have five horses. Said she was sure Trixie would keep Susie exercised when she was too busy to ride." He glared across the table at Trixie. "That's gratitude for you. I suppose, now that you and Honey are loaded with money, you wouldn't consider buying the little mare and giving her to Miss Trask. Miss Trask, the best friend you ever had!"

Trixie's mouth fell open with surprise. "B-But, Re-Regan," she stuttered. "I don't know what you're talking about. I haven't enough money to buy a horse. In fact, I owe Tom Delanoy fifty cents."

"I paid him for you," Brian said. "Did Honey tell you that he starts work out here as chauffeur after Labor Day?"

"I was there when she interviewed Tom," Trixie replied. "You'll like him a lot, Regan. And please, don't be so mysterious. What made you say that Honey and I are loaded with money?"

Regan pushed back his chair and stood up. "You can't sit there and tell me that there wasn't a fat reward offered for the recovery of that diamond! Fat enough, anyway, to convince Jed Tomlin that Susie ought to stay on here." He glared at Trixie again, his mouth twitching as he tried not to smile. "If you don't buy that mare for Miss Trask, Trixie Belden, I'll never let you put your foot in my stable again." He strode out and the screen door slammed behind him.

Trixie reached weakly across the table to clutch Honey's hands. "Oh, oh," they cried together. "Oh, *oh, OH!*"

"Oh, brother," Mart crowed. "Five horses for five mounted Bob-Whites of the Glen. And all of them always needing exercise!"

"It's the answer to everything, all right," Jim said.

"It certainly is," Brian said with a grin. "Now that Trixie doesn't have to save up for that colt any more, she can contribute every cent she earns toward the clubhouse."

"I will," Trixie said. "And I've got twenty-five dollars in the savings bank. We should be able to put on a new roof for that."

Mart flung his arm around her shoulders and hugged her. "You're a great girl, Trix," he said softly. "Super! Even if you can't thread a needle, I wouldn't swap you for any other sister in the world."

"And Mars," Brian added. "The whole universe, in fact. There never was anyone like Trixie, and I guess there never will be!"